THE PANTY MELTER

LILI VALENTE

❀ Created with Vellum

THE PANTY MELTER

By Lili Valente

ABOUT THE BOOK

I don't date alpha males.

Especially not alpha males with egos the size of Jupiter, who also happen to be my boss's big brother.

Deacon Hunter is domineering. Condescending. *Infuriating.*

And yet I can't seem to keep my panties on for five minutes when we're alone together.

He keeps melting them right off. With that sexy voice, those confident hands, the way he brings my body wildly to life, he's proved my libido hasn't gone into permanent, post-divorce hibernation after all.

Surely there's no harm in being enemies with benefits... Right?

When Violet Boden asks me to take her Divorce Virginity, the only thing I can think is—come again?

No, seriously, *come again.*

And again and again, until both of us are so satisfied we can't remember the people who did us wrong.

Best if we keep conversation to a minimum, though, considering I drive her crazy. She drives me crazy sometimes, too. But she's also sweet, loyal, fearless, and so much fun she's making it damn hard not to fall for her.

But how to convince a woman who's put me in the emotional no-fly zone that I deserve a place in her heart?

ALSO BY LILI VALENTE

Laugh-out-Loud Rocker Rom Coms

The Bangover

Bang Theory

Banging The Enemy

The Rock Star's Baby Bargain

Hometown Heat Series

All Fired Up

Catching Fire

Playing with Fire

A Little Less Conversation

The Bliss River Small Town Series

Falling for the Fling

Falling for the Ex

Falling for the Bad Boy

The Hunter Brothers

The Baby Maker

The Troublemaker

The Heartbreaker

The Panty Melter

Big O Dating Specialists
Romantic Comedies

Hot Revenge for Hire

Hot Knight for Hire

Hot Mess for Hire

Hot Ghosthunter for Hire

The Lonesome Point Series

(Sexy Cowboys)

Leather and Lace
Saddles and Sin
Diamonds and Dust
12 Dates of Christmas
Glitter and Grit
Sunny with a Chance of True Love
Chaps and Chance
Ropes and Revenge
8 Second Angel

The Good Love Series
(co-written with Lauren Blakely)
The V Card
Good with His Hands
Good to be Bad

The Happy Cat Series
(co-written with Pippa Grant)
Hosed
Hammered
Hitched
Humbugged

PROLOGUE

THE PANTY MELTER

*O*ne shot.

That's all you get.

One chance at a love that lasts.

Maybe two, if you're really lucky or really stupid or really good at forgetting how bad love roughed you up the first time.

Me? I've got a memory a mile long. My heart is an elephant that never forgets. Every miserable moment of my failed first shot at love is tattooed on my soul, lodged so deep in the wrinkles of my brain I couldn't pull them out if I tried.

But why would I want to do something like that?

I like to learn from my mistakes, and to do that, I need to remember them. You know what they say—fool me once, shame on you, but fool me twice...

I'm nobody's fool, especially Love's. That's why I keep things casual, physical. I'll make you come so hard you'll forget your own name, but I'm not coming home to meet the folks. I've got enough on my plate with my

1

own crazy family; I don't need a booster shot of nuts from yours.

Especially when we both know it's not going to last.

Chemistry fizzles, love fades, and happily-ever-after is the stuff of fairy tales. The only thing you can count on is this moment, this breath, this chance to choose pleasure over pain, to make love instead of ill-advised romantic declarations you'll regret when the hormone rush fades away.

I know these things to be true.

They might as well be tattooed next to the pin-up girl I got inked on my shoulder during my first deployment.

But as I guide Violet Boden to the dusty floor of the attic at the Morton's annual Halloween party—lips fused, breath coming fast, and hands everywhere, all at once—I'm possessed by the certainty that everything is about to change. There's something on the wind, in the honeysuckle and sage scent of her perfume, in the way her hands tremble as she threads her fingers into my hair and holds on for dear life as I make her come with my mouth.

Again.

And again.

And then one more time because I can't get enough of the sexy sounds she makes and the sweet taste of her body and the warm rush of her pleasure soaking through my skin to settle in my bones. It just feels so good, so fucking right that I want to stay with her in this attic forever, to die getting each other off and haunt it together as hedonistic ghosts.

I've been a Panty Melter for as long as I can

remember—I know what I'm doing between the sheets and have never had any trouble getting a woman out of her clothes and into my bed—but I'm usually ready to make tracks the moment things threaten to get heavy.

But when Violet kisses me with tears in her eyes, the intimate taste of her mingling with the rum and coke lingering on her lips, and says, "Thank you, Sexy Stranger. I didn't think I'd ever feel that way again. It had been so long," I don't want to bolt. I want to stay, kiss away her tears, and make her happy all over again—this time with my cock instead of my mouth.

"I don't have a condom, but I'm shooting blanks, and I'm clean." I cup her breast in my hand, rolling her perfect bud of a nipple between my finger and thumb. "And I would really love to be inside you."

"Yes," she breathes, rubbing my erection through the thin fabric of my costume pants. For the fourth year in a row, I'm dressed as Westley from *The Princess Bride*, complete with a fencing sword that I tossed aside a good twenty minutes ago.

There's only one sword on my mind at the moment...

"But I want to see you," Violet continues, reaching for the knot holding my mask in place.

And yes, I'm wearing a mask.

And yes, it covers all of my hair and half of my face.

And yes, Violet and I are relatively new acquaintances, only having met once before this party, when I stopped by the shelter where she works to let my brother, her boss, know that his pet cow was knocked up.

So it's not all that hard to see how she could have

mistaken me for someone else. But when she pulls off the mask, her eyes widening in horror as recognition apparently dawns, I'm still thrown for a loop.

"Deacon? Oh my God." She scrambles backward across the dusty boards, fumbling for her discarded genie pantaloons with a frantic hand. "Oh my God."

"Is something wrong?" I ask, wincing as I adjust my equally confused cock.

"You. This. Me." She shakes her head as she jabs one foot into her pants and then the other, jerking them up around her hips with a rush of breath. "We can't do this. No way. If I'd known who you were, I never would have—" She cuts off with a laugh that stings a little. "Oh my God, this is crazy."

"You seriously didn't know who I was?"

Her eyes bulge. "Why do you think I kept calling you Sexy Stranger?"

"Role-playing? For fun?"

She huffs. "I don't role-play on a first date. Or first hookup. Or whatever this was." She winces. "I don't do this at all. Ever. I must have been out of my mind." She backs away, hands flapping at her sides. "I'm sorry. Please, let's just forget this ever happened. Okay? Thanks. Sorry. God. Bye."

Before I can say a word, she dashes across the drafty room and disappears down the secret staircase, leaving me holding my own sword and feeling like an asshat for letting "this could be something special" thoughts knock around inside my skull.

Tonight wasn't special, and nothing is going to change. Violet Boden clearly likes me about as much as she enjoys razor blades in her Halloween candy, and I can't say I'm too fond of her right now, either.

But as I head back to the party, I can't get her smell, her taste, her touch out of my head.

I go home, lie in bed alone, and jerk off to memories of her writhing beneath me, but it doesn't help. I pass a restless night plagued by erotic dreams of Ms. Boden until a call from my youngest brother, Tristan, wakes me up the next morning so he can announce he's decided to get married in his backyard.

Today. Immediately.

And guess who's officiating the service?

That's right—Violet, wearing a skimpy sundress with no bra and acting as if nothing happened between us.

She's cool, distant, and so fucking sexy I can't keep my eyes off of her.

I spend the ceremony hiding a semi behind my crossed arms and bad attitude and spend the after-party as far from the object of my erotic frustration as possible. I leave early, heading to a dive bar to drink the insufferable woman off my mind.

Only I'm not sure there's enough whiskey in the world to numb the sting of the cold shoulder she gave me today—or how damn much I still want her in spite of it.

CHAPTER 1

VIOLET

$\mathcal{T}$he only thing worse than being stood up by your first-ever Blender-app date in front of two of your closest friends?

Being stood up in front of your friends after having spent the previous evening regretting an ill-advised make-out session, and the day officiating the most romantic wedding ever.

I just married two people who are joyfully wallowing in the kind of love I'll never have again. The kind of love I probably *never* had. After all, if the love had been real, my ex wouldn't have run off with his secretary and left me with three girls to raise on my own.

And yes, Grant pays child support.

And yes, he shows up every other weekend for visitation.

And yes, he's a decent human being, and most days I would call us friends and effective co-parents who nailed the amicable divorce routine and stuck the landing.

But today I want to wrap my hands around Grant's muscly neck and squeeze until his stupid tongue flops out. Today, I'm feeling everything I lost all over again—all raw and sad and awful.

Even after two years of the new normal, it still hurts so much sometimes. To remember how safe and loved I felt. To remember how certain I'd been that I was smack-dab in the middle of happily-ever-after. I'd been so sure that the loving family Grant and I had made with our girls was the one thing in this crazy, mixed-up world I could count on.

And then all that certainty vanished. Instantly, in the heartbeat between Grant's tortured, "There's something I have to tell you, Violet," and the moment the bomb dropped.

That's what I called her at first.

The bomb.

It's fitting. Tracey might be a twit with a brain the size of a shriveled persimmon, but she's a bombshell. Flawless. Perfect from her halo of blond curls and her crystal-clear blue eyes to the oddly tiny feet holding up all five feet ten inches of her willowy, yet impossibly big-breasted, frame.

And the boobs are real. Which is worse, somehow, isn't it? More unfair than if they'd been purchased at a plastic surgeon's office and tacked on to all that other perfection at a later date.

I glance down at my pink and orange slip dress, the one I absolutely do *not* need to wear a bra with to keep the girls contained, and wonder for the thousandth time if it was my nearly flat-chested state that drove Grant into the arms of another woman.

But deep down I know my itty-bitties had nothing to do with it. Grant has a thing for younger women. Once upon a time, *I* was the barely legal girl who caught his eye, the dumb kid who got knocked up on our third date and had been so grateful that Grant was willing to try to make it work with a starving artist for a wife.

Now I'm newly forty. Still only making art part-time. Barely dating at all. And having no sex, not even bad sex, because the men I've been barely dating are awful or mean or weird in gross and unattractive ways. Oh, and being publicly stood up on a street corner because, once again, I've managed to go bobbing for apples and pluck a wormy one from the bottom of the barrel.

Silently, I wish Chad67 chronic erectile dysfunction and a nasty case of shingles and force a smile.

"Welp. That's it!" I clench my jaw to keep my grin in place as Mary and Virginia, my work buddies, wince sympathetically in my direction. "He's clearly not coming, so I'm going to buy two pints of ice cream and head home to binge-watch House Hunters International. You guys have fun at your concert."

"Oh, honey," Mary murmurs. "I'm sorry."

I shrug a breezy shoulder. "So I got stood up. It's fine. I'm totally fine."

"Better than fine," Virginia agrees with a nod that makes her gray ponytail twitch. "I'm telling you Violet, males of the species are more trouble than they're worth. You'll see."

Mary and Virginia have been volunteering at the animal shelter where I work for fifteen years and are some of my sweetest old friends. They're both in their sixties and gave up dating many moons ago. They assure me I'm going to love being older and alone. Apparently, as soon as my sex drive sputters out, life will be all smooth sailing, bingo nights, wine tasting with girl-friends, and long walks through the redwoods with no one droning on and on in a big stupid man voice, disturbing the peace.

It sounds amazing.

So amazing that the back of my nose begins to sting and tears stab into my eyes as I contemplate a life with no kisses in it. No snuggles into shirts that smell like smoky cologne. No more catching someone's eye across the room and knowing the smirk that curves his lips is just for me.

And, of course, no more orgasms that don't come courtesy of my battery operated boyfriend. Last night with Deacon was a mistake—a huge, terrible, awful, no-good mistake—for so many reasons, but the worst part is that he reminded me of all the things I'm missing. Things like human touch and kisses and pleasure and orgasms.

God, there were so many orgasms...

I've missed them so much. No vibrator on earth can hold a candle to a man's mouth, a man's hands, a man's—

Nope. I shake my head firmly. I'm not going to think about that.

Deacon was a mistake I won't be repeating, and the rest of Sonoma County's single men are more trouble than they're worth. I'm just going to have to get used to a life without cock. A cockless, solitary, lone-vagina-against-the-world existence.

I can't stop a pathetic little sob that makes both my

self-appointed chaperones coo with concern as they close ranks around me.

"Oh, sweetheart. Come here. Ugh. I could just kick that jerk in the face!" Mary gathers me into her arms, crushing me against her ample bosom, proving that even the big-breasted among us can get tossed aside. Mary's husband left her when she was thirty-eight, too, right after she gave birth to their second child.

"That's not where I'd kick him. I'd aim lower," Virginia mutters, making me laugh.

I step away from Mary with a sniff, determined to pull myself together. "You guys are the best. You want to hit bingo night at the Sisters of Mercy next week? It's still on Wednesday nights, right?"

Mary's eyes light up, and her furrowed brow relaxes. "It is! And I've got a new selection of lucky hats! Enough for all of us. Bring Adriana, she'll love them."

I ignore the fresh pang of sadness that flashes through my chest at the mention of my youngest daughter. "I'll try, but she's been so busy with track and all her senior activities I barely see her anymore. She might be too cool for bingo these days."

"No one's ever too cool for bingo," Mary scoffs. "She'll come. She won't be able to resist. Deep down, she's still the same kid who brought her troll dolls to the VA Bingo Tournament and lined up red jellybeans along the top of her cards for good luck. You'll see."

I smile, hoping she's right. "I'll try to talk her into it. But you two should get going. Doesn't the concert start soon? If you don't hurry, you won't find parking."

"They're sold out, or we'd offer to bring you along," Virginia says.

"But we can be late if you need us to stay." Mary casts a glance up and down the street in front of Oakville Grocery, where Chad67 and I were supposed to meet. It's still a good hour until dark, with plenty of people out enjoying the warm Indian summer night, but Mary's a worrier from way back. "I hate to leave you here alone. Do you need us to walk you to your car?"

"No, thank you," I say. "I'm fine."

"Or you could take my ticket," Mary says, her eyes lighting up as inspiration strikes. "I don't mind. I'm leaving for my Alaskan cruise next weekend, so I should get home and start packing anyway."

"No way, crazy! I'm not taking your ticket." I shoo them off. "I'm fine to get home by myself. You two go. Have fun. It's been a big day, and I'm honestly relieved for an excuse to get in my pajamas."

"Well, if you're sure." Mary hedges back a step, tugged along by Virginia, who hasn't missed a Rockin' the Vines performance at Sampson's Point Vineyard in ten years.

I continue to insist that I *am* sure as they turn toward Mary's car, and Virginia calls over her shoulder, "Remember—don't let the bastards grind you down!"

I hide my wince behind a wave as they buckle in and roll out onto Matheson Street, headed toward the highway. Only when they're out of sight do I let my arm drop heavily to my side and my shoulders slump.

Time to head home.

Home. It's the same house I shared with Grant when we were married, the one the girls and I have made a true, pink-celebrating, lady-lair in the past two years, but it doesn't feel as cozy as it used to. Emily and Beatrice, my two oldest, are both away at college and living in the dorms. It's just Addie and me at home, and she's out with friends tonight, staying over at a hotel in Vallejo so they can hit the amusement park nearby first thing in the morning.

That's the reason I arranged to meet Chad the Douchebag tonight in the first place—so I wouldn't have to go home to a lonely house after the wedding and eat a depressing dinner for one in front of the TV.

And so I wouldn't be tempted by a certain brooding alpha male…

Deacon looks way too good in a suit, so good a girl could forget that he's her boss's big brother and way too much like her ex-husband to make dating him a wise choice. I'm finished with bossy, domineering, love-em-and-leave-em men. I'm going to find a nice man who checks all the boxes on my relationship wish list or die alone.

"I don't want to be alone," I murmur to a miniature poodle tied up outside a wine-tasting room near the grocery. She barks if to say, "It could be worse, woman. You could be chained up on a gum-pocked sidewalk while your owners get wasted. At least you've got your freedom."

"True," I agree, pulling my cell from my purse. The poodle is right. I've got free will, and it's not too late to turn this night around.

I shoot my friend Mina—my only single girlfriend—a text to see if she might be up for a spontaneous girls' night, but she almost instantly shoots back—*Sorry. Can't. On a date with one of my hot babies.*

My nose wrinkles as I tap out, *How old is this one? Twenty-eight?*

Twenty-seven! Her enthusiastic response is accompanied by a winking emoji, a kiss-blowing emoji, and a string of perky-looking eggplants.

I roll my eyes, encourage her to *Have fun,* and drop my phone back into my purse.

At least someone is enjoying themselves tonight. And getting laid, even if it is by a man twelve years her junior.

But Mina insists the only available men are either a decade younger or a decade older, and from what little dating I've done, I'm afraid she's right. I don't know what the men around our age are doing—staying happily married or dating girls young enough to be their children or having such debilitating mid-life crises they're unable to drag themselves out of the house after work—but they are in shockingly short supply.

Most of the men I've gone out with have been in their fifties and already working on a middle-aged paunch and a grouchy old man attitude. A little cushion around the middle, I don't mind, but being snapped at every time I accidentally disrupt a guy's rigid, aging-single-dude routine isn't something I enjoy.

I have three hormonal daughters to snap at me, thank you very much.

Maybe I should give younger men a chance—Mina certainly seems to be enjoying her shameless sampling of the twenty-five to thirty-year-old men of Sonoma County—but I can't help but wish for something more.

For someone closer to my age, who understands where I'm coming from, who's been knocked around by life enough to appreciate little blessings and everyday miracles. Someone who has something on his mind aside from how quickly he can get me out of my clothes and into his bed.

Because I'm not into one-night stands.

Or I wasn't into them.

Until last night, when I almost banged Deacon in a stranger's attic.

Though, of course, I didn't *know* he was Deacon at the time. I thought I was banging a *complete stranger* in a stranger's attic, which makes the entire thing even worse.

But if I hadn't whipped off his mask and revealed his true, off-limits identity, I wouldn't have stopped. I was out of my mind with wanting him, possessed by a wild lust monster clawing away beneath my skin, desperate to rip free and devour everything in its path—namely, all six feet two inches of Deacon Hunter's magically delicious body.

The man is mind-bendingly fun to look at, with sky blue eyes, the broadest shoulders I've ever seen, abs of pure titanium, and powerful calloused hands that knew exactly how to touch me without a word of direction.

It's eighty degrees outside, but still I shiver, my nipples pulling tight against the silky fabric of my dress as I start across the street, not sure where I'm going, but needing to move, to burn off some of this restless, pulsing energy.

I want to go back there, to that dusty room with the stranger in the mask, to that moment before I peeled away the fabric covering Deacon's face, and this time keep going. I want to know what it feels like to have him inside me more than I want air.

Definitely more than I want dinner from Oakville Grocery or those two pints of ice cream.

I'm not hungry for food, I'm starved for touch, for skin on skin, for Deacon's lips hot on mine, and his hand sliding down the front of my panties.

No, not Deacon. The stranger. *That's* who I want. The stranger, who isn't tangled up in a web of complex interpersonal connections. Deacon's brother, Tristan, is not only my boss, he just married one of my best friends. And the other Hunter brothers, Dylan and Rafe, have been in my life for years. Sometimes I even babysit Dylan's daughter when his usual sitter is out of town. In a lot of ways, they're like family.

And you don't roll around naked in an attic with your family's family, even if the man in question has been working outside the country so much the past twenty years that you barely know him.

I know enough to realize it would never work, even if he weren't a Hunter.

Deacon spent twenty-five years in the military; I'm a pacifist who's never shot a spitball, let alone a gun. Deacon is a logical rule follower; I'm a mischief-maker who lets my heart be my guide. Most importantly, Deacon is a bossy alpha male with too much testosterone for his own good, and I want no part of that. Not again.

I barely survived that the first time.

When Grant left, he didn't just break my heart, he left me scrambling to learn how to pay the bills, renew the car insurance, stick to a budget, and all the other things he'd exercised complete control of during our marriage. It was terrifying, the constant worry that I was going to make a mistake and my kids would end up sleeping in a dark, cold house because I'd let the electricity get turned off.

I'm in control now, and that's the way it's going to stay.

But that doesn't mean I can't let loose once in a while, especially when there's no one waiting at home...

I slow at the next corner, ears pricking as I catch a few notes of the song playing inside the bar across the street. It's a hole in the wall I've never been in before, but I'd recognize the bass line of Heart's *Magic Man* anywhere, and it's been way too long since I've been dancing.

Dancing is in my blood, in my soul, the only thing that lights me up as much as throwing pottery. It's also an excellent way to burn off excess energy, the kind that might tempt a girl to do something stupid like call the guy she almost banged last night and ask if he might be up for finishing the job...

Without another thought, I hurry across the street and push through the creaky door into the murky light inside, heading straight for the small, mostly abandoned dance floor.

I'm not afraid to dance alone.

I do everything alone these days, why should dancing be any different?

CHAPTER 2

DEACON

The minute the bombshell with the silky black hair down to her ass walks into the bar, I know there's going to be trouble. And then she starts dancing—spinning around in her sexy-as-hell dress, her hair swirling and twitching around her hips as she swivels in time with the song wailing from the jukebox —and every muscle in my body tenses.

I'm instantly on high alert, hyperaware of every male eye in the joint turning to watch Violet Boden like she's a baby gazelle that just wandered out into the open savanna.

Because she isn't just any bombshell.

She's *my* bombshell.

Or she almost was, anyway. We got so close to sealing the deal last night that I haven't been able to think of anything else all day. In body, I was standing up at my brother's wedding, but in spirit I was back with Violet in the moonlight, with my mouth between her legs and my heart slamming inside my chest, hearing those sexy gasps and moans that drove me out of my mind with wanting her.

I jerked off twice last night and once this morning, like a teenager with his first boner, but she's still in my head. I'm thicker than I was a moment ago, and if I don't get her off the dance floor, the situation below my belt is going to get downright embarrassing.

And this evening could get dangerous. For her.

There are some unsavory patrons here tonight.

The Raven's Claw is the last true dive bar left in Healdsburg, maybe in all of Sonoma County. They only accept cash, the clientele is composed mainly of grizzled bikers and vets old enough to have fought in 'Nam, and the grimy dance floor has probably never seen a woman as pretty as Violet Boden.

God, she's stunning. And still *not* wearing a bra, a fact I'm sure hasn't escaped the attention of perverts old enough to be her father.

The thought is barely through my head when Benji, a Vietnam Vet with a glass eye and a swollen foot he swears is just naturally twice the size of his other one and not a sign of advanced Deep Vein Thrombosis, heaves himself off his stool and makes a beeline for Violet like a sex-goddess-seeking missile.

Benji is harmless—he might talk Violet's leg off, but he wouldn't lay a hand on her—but the man swaggering onto the floor to her left could be trouble. He's probably thirty, but looks older, his thin chest hollowed out by too much drink. He's got a hungry look in his eyes that makes me want to throw my jacket around Violet and hustle her outside. I don't recognize him, and I've been coming to the Claw since my dad used to drag me in here for harvest parties when I was still too young to drink.

But of course, I did drink.

Willa, the former owner and bartender, had a soft spot for young guys. Ten minutes of flashing my seventeen-year-old dimples in her direction and I was set up with a Coke spiked so hard I was usually seeing double by the time I left. I credit Willa—and an especially wicked hangover the day after my eighteenth birthday—for my continued aversion to gin.

I've got a history with this place, these people, one that usually affords a certain amount of respect for anyone I bring in with me, which means it's time to make it clear Violet is under my protection.

Setting my beer on the bar, I slide off my stool and stride purposefully across the room, reaching Violet seconds before Hollow Chest and closing my fingers around her wrist.

She flinches in surprise, and her half-closed lids open wide.

I lean down, letting my lips linger near her ear, inhaling the salty-sweet smell of her as I whisper, "You shouldn't come into a place like this alone. It's not safe."

She huffs as she pulls her arm away. "This is Healdsburg, not the mean streets of Shanghai. I can take care of myself, thanks."

"I'm not so sure about that." I stand my ground at the edge of the dance floor as she starts to sway once more.

"Well, I am." She flutters her fingers as she lifts her arms over her head. "I appreciate the concern, but I'm just fine."

I nod. "All right. I'll be back when you get into trouble."

Irritation flashes in her eyes. "That was patronizing."

"Wasn't intended to be. Just stating the facts." I turn on my heel and return to my stool, ignoring the stinging sensation at the back of my neck. That's just wounded pride. The first woman I've made out with since getting out of the service four months ago runs in horror when she realizes we aren't strangers? That was not fun.

In fact, it pretty much sucked all the ass. I'd been certain Violet knew who I was from the beginning and that the "sexy stranger" talk was just part of the fun.

And we *were* having fun. She can give me the cold shoulder all she wants today, but we both know that last night I set her on fire.

"Don't think about last night," I mutter, motioning to Toby, the bartender, for another beer.

I will not think about Violet's breasts arching toward the ceiling while I devoured her pussy. I will not think about her fingers tangled in my hair or her sweet taste filling my mouth or the way she moaned in anticipation as she rubbed my cock through my jeans.

And I'm certainly not going to turn and watch her dance.

I don't need to look at her. I'll know when she's in trouble. I'll be able to feel the change in the energy of the room, the shift in the wind as potential danger becomes something I need to worry about. Years of training and multiple deployments to war zones have given me a sixth sense when it comes to trouble.

Too bad I don't always listen to it...

"You know her?" Toby asks, nodding toward the dance floor as he sets down my pale ale.

"I do." And I knew she was trouble the moment I laid eyes on her. But I still danced with her, flirted with her, and led her up to a secret place where we could be alone because opposites attract.

Until they start to irritate the shit out of each other. Say, when one of them insists on putting herself in danger for absolutely no reason except that she refuses to listen to the voice of reason, for example.

"She's something else." Toby's graying eyebrows lift higher on his forehead. "Makes me wish Baxter was in tonight. Always nice to have an off-duty cop around. Just in case."

I grunt in agreement. "I'm concerned about the new guy. The one in the blue T-shirt and flannel."

"You should be. He's been drinking whiskey since four o'clock, and Cassie already had to give him an earful about an hour ago. He wouldn't let up with Becca, even after she told him repeatedly that she likes girls and was here with her partner."

"I'm sure Cassie made him regret that." Cassie is only five three, but she was a Marine for ten years. She's tough as nails and fiercely protective of her girlfriend.

Toby chuckles. "He slunk away with his tail tucked between his legs pretty tight. Thought he was out of here, but guess he just went out for a smoke. He definitely perked up when your gypsy walked in." He glances past me, amusement flickering in his eyes.

"Though, looks like Benji's giving him a run for his money."

I swivel on my stool to see Violet twirling under Benji's arm, laughing at something he's just said like they've been friends for years. For his part, Old Benj is beaming, his round face flushed bright red. He continues to dance—badly—while talking Violet's leg off in a voice not quite loud enough to be heard over the music.

The Heart song ends, and a Led Zeppelin classic takes its place, and still Benji and Violet are swaying hand in hand, apparently getting on like a house on fire, while the creep in the flannel prowls the edge of the dance floor, looking for an opening that's not coming. I'm starting to think everything might be all right, when Benji cringes, his spine stiffening as he reaches down to clutch his right knee.

Violet lays a gentle hand on his back, clearly concerned, and murmurs something close to his ear. Benji shakes his head with a pained smile and motions toward the back hallway, where a single unisex toilet serves as the john for the entire bar. Violet tries to follow as he hobbles away, but Benji waves her off. Whether he's faking the need for a bathroom break to cover for his bad knee or really has to take a leak, it doesn't matter.

All that matters is that Violet is alone on the dance floor, and Hollow Chest is clear to make his move. I see it coming—the inevitable conflict as he tries to take Benji's place and oversteps himself—and my gut shouts for me to step in before it's too late.

But Violet made it clear she doesn't want any trouble

repellent, at least not if it's coming from me. So I clench my jaw and keep my ass in my seat as the creep slithers a hand around Violet's waist, pulling her too close. She spins away with a laugh, subtly making it clear she isn't interested in a slow dance, but the asshole just moves in again, backing her into a corner by the jukebox and reaching for her hair, proving he isn't interested in respecting her space.

She dodges his grasping fingers, discomfort and fear mixing in her features, but still I sit. I wait, curling my hands into fists on my thighs as the handsy bastard grabs a fistful of her dress, holding her prisoner as she tries to dart around him. Violet shoves at his arm, her eyes bright and angry, and Hollow Chest responds with a mean laugh as he braces a hand on the wall behind her.

Every cell in my body is screaming for me to get over there, rip the guy's hands off of her and stuff them into his mouth, but I'm not going anywhere until I get the signal.

The sign I'm waiting for.

The one I know is coming in three…

Two….

Violet's head turns sharply to the right, her frightened eyes seeking mine across the bar, and I'm out of my seat in one hot second. The next, I'm behind the creep, hand curled tight around his shoulder.

"Hands off. Now." I dig my fingers tighter into his bony flesh, silently promising him that I'm only going to ask nicely once.

He wheels around to face me, eyes narrow and a sneer on his lips that falls away when he gets a good look at who he's about to start a fight with. All of the men in my family are tall and solidly built, and for twenty years the weight room has been my second home. Exercise is my therapy, one that doesn't cost a dime and keeps me in the kind of condition that ends most fights before they get started.

Unless they're really drunk or really stupid, most men know better than to mess with a guy who's got fifty pounds of pure muscle on them and a "don't fuck with me" look in his eye.

Hollow Chest is drunk—I can smell the cheap whiskey in his sweat—but he isn't drunk enough to start something that's going to end with him unconscious on the floor.

"Didn't realize she was spoken for, man," he says, sidling away toward the jukebox. "You should keep a tighter leash on your lady."

"I'm not—" Violet begins, but I cut her off with a sharp—

"And you should learn to keep your hands to yourself. Now leave. And don't come back. This isn't the bar for you. We don't like your kind of asshole."

"Yeah, only our kind of asshole!" George, a seriously bearded biker, shouts from the nearby pool table, inspiring laughter in the rest of the men gathered around the cues.

For a second, Hollow Chest looks like he's going to pop off to George—which would be a much bigger mistake than running off his mouth at me, seeing as George hits first and asks questions never.

But apparently, this loser isn't stupid, either.

In the end, he scrubs a hand over his clenched jaw,

mutters something unintelligible beneath his breath, and slinks out the door, letting in a rosy flash of sunset on his way out. The warm glow lights up Violet's pale face, making her look like a model from one of those old Italian paintings my first stepmom loves so much, and then darkness falls again, leaving us alone in the shadows.

After a long beat, she clears her throat. "Thank you."

"You're welcome." I try not to sound smug, but do a shit job of it, so I'm not really surprised when irritation flashes across her features again.

"Go ahead and say 'I told you' so if it'll make you feel better."

"I feel just fine," I say. But I don't. I'm feverish, hungry, starved to the bone for another taste of Violet's mouth. I'm out of my head with wanting this woman. It's the only explanation for the words that come tumbling out of my mouth, seeing as I'm not usually a glutton for punishment. "Though, I'd like to know why you ran away last night. I thought we were having a good time. I know I was."

Her lashes flutter. "Last night was a mistake. We're not a good fit, Deacon."

"How do you figure? You barely know me."

"I know your type," she says, crossing her arms. "And I know a lot of women are into the controlling alpha-male thing, but I'm not."

I frown so hard my nostrils flare. "Controlling alpha male? Where the hell did you get that?"

"From the way you walk, the way you talk, the way you boss your family around." She motions toward the dance floor. "The way you decide what's best for complete strangers and rush in shouting orders."

"I wasn't shouting. Or rushing. And you weren't safe." I point toward the door her harasser exited less than two minutes ago. "Clearly. I wasn't controlling, I was protecting. And as far as—"

"I don't need protecting," she pops back, lifting her chin.

"Pardon my French, but I'm going to have to call bullshit on that, Ms. Boden," I say, leaning closer to her stubborn little mouth. "You need a bodyguard almost as much as you need a shot of common sense."

Her eyes flash. "I can't believe I got naked with you."

"You got naked with me because I drive you crazy," I murmur, blood pumping faster as her nipples tighten, poking through the thin fabric of her dress. "Hell, I'm driving you crazy right now."

"I can't stand you," she says in a breathy voice that goes straight to my stiffening cock.

"But you still want to kiss me," I whisper.

"I want lots of stupid things," she says, her hands reaching for my chest.

I'm certain she's going to push me away, so certain that I'm already braced to catch myself with a quick step back. Instead, she fists her hands in my shirt, hauling me close as she presses up on tiptoe, fusing her lips to mine.

The kiss is instantly hot, wild, and completely inappropriate for public consumption. I'm dimly aware of hoots and cheers coming from the other patrons as Violet's tongue sweeps into my mouth, but it's hard to focus on anything but the rush of attraction, the electric feel of her hands smoothing around to grip my shoulders, the spike of arousal coursing through me as her curves press against my chest.

I know we should stop, or at least take this outside, but my brain can't talk my body into cooperating. I'm too lost in this woman, helpless in the face of a firestorm of attraction even hotter than the one that raged between us last night.

Finally, she pulls away, panting against my lips, "I'm going home now."

"Is that an invitation?"

"No. We're not going to do this. We're going to be friends. Just friends."

"I don't want to be your friend."

"Good," she says with a sniff. "I don't want to be your friend, either." And then she kisses me again—hard and deep—before making a beeline for the door and slamming out into the evening air without a backward glance.

I'm about to go after her when the door opens and Violet pops her head back in, pointing a stern finger my way. "Don't follow me."

She vanishes again, leaving me with the laughter of the assembled company. A beat later, Benji appears at my side, clapping a hand on my back. "It's okay, man. Some wild horses just can't be broken."

"I don't want to break her; I want to date her," I hear myself saying. I'm not sure where the words came from —I don't want to date her, I find her every bit as frustrating as she finds me—but still…

There's something about her…

Something that makes me sneak to the door and

glance outside, just to make sure Hollow Chest isn't giving her trouble on her way to her car. He isn't. There's no sign of him, only a firecracker in a dress all the colors of the sun, running away from me as fast as her shapely legs can carry her.

CHAPTER 3

From the texts of Violet Boden and
Mina Smalls

Violet: Are you awake? I desperately need advice, and there's no one else I can ask.

Mina: Yeah, I'm up, but what can possibly be so desperate at six a.m. on a Sunday?

Violet: I need you to tell me how to turn my libido off. The way you did when you swore off sex last Christmas, remember?

Mina: Um, yes, I do…but why would you want to do that? Sex is fun and you definitely need to get laid, Vi. How long has it been since the divorce?
A year and a half?

Violet: Two years. Six weeks.

Mina: HOLY SHIT! How has that much time passed already? It seems like you guys just split up!

Violet: It's because we're old. Time flies when you're getting old.

Mina: Speak for yourself, honey. I'm feeling amazingly youthful and vibrant this morning. Especially considering I didn't get to sleep until two a.m. Hot babies don't require sleep. They can survive on energy drinks, ramen, and sex alone. Or probably just sex and the occasional glass of water to replenish all those lost bodily fluids.

Violet: Stop! I don't want to talk about sex or hot babies or bodily fluids. I want to talk about winter landscapes covered in fallen snow and bare tree limbs and still, quiet darkness without a speck of light.

Mina: That sounds as depressing as hell. Who has you so upset, mama? Tell me his name. I'll kick him in the balls for you.

Violet: I don't want you to kick him in the balls, I just want to forget about his balls and his lips and his hands and the way the smell of him makes my mouth water like a ravenous sex monster.

Mina: Oooo! A ravenous sex monster! That sounds like fun. You should go for it! Ravage him, girl. Tear his clothes off and have your wicked way with him.

Violet: You're not listening.

Mina: No, you're not listening. It's time to come out of hiding, Violet. You've mourned long enough. It's time to get back in the saddle and ride this stallion who has you so worked up. Ride him all night long, girl!

Violet: I can't! He's a jerk with an ego the size of Tracey's enormous boobs, and I refuse to lose my Divorce Virginity to an asshole.

Mina: I hear you. Mean people are the worst. And you can't reward that kind of behavior with pussy, or they'll never learn.

Violet: He's not mean, exactly, just...bossy. And controlling. And insufferable. But for some reason, I can't stop thinking about him and fantasizing about him and wanting his big stupid hands all over me. I barely slept at all last night. It's like I've been infected with some sort of terrible disease, Mina. You've got to help me!

Mina: No, no, no. It's not a disease, darlin'. That's just your lady beast, ready to come out and rule the night! And we don't want to put her to sleep. We just need to point her claws in another direction.

Violet: I tried that, but that guy I've been texting on Blender stood me up.

Mina: Well, I can't say I'm surprised. That's what you get for trying to hook up with someone named Chad.

Violet: What's wrong with the name Chad?

Mina: Chads are all pasty, weak-willed, whiny, overly entitled rich white guys who think their shit doesn't stink and their tiny cocks are God's gift to women.

Violet: That's harsh. But…maybe kind of accurate, now that I think about it.

Mina: I once named a hemorrhoid Chad. That's all that name is good for.

Violet: LOL. You're insane.

Mina: Agreed. But I'm also here for you, and I've got an extra ticket to the River and Blues festival this afternoon. You should come with me, drink a few beers, listen to some good music, and see if any of the shirtless men catch your inner wild cat's fancy. If all goes well, we could have you happily boinking a hot baby of your own before sunset.

Violet: I don't think I want a hot baby.

Mina: Okay, fine, then you can scope out a sexy silver fox and leave all the hot babies for me. I find that a more than acceptable arrangement. I'd forgotten how nice it is to be able to get a guy hard with nothing but a wink and a smile. Getting my ex in the mood was such a production I was exhausted before we even got started.

Violet: Grant never had problems with that.

Mina: We're not talking about Grant or thinking about Grant. Grant is the past. The smoking-hot single men of Sonoma County are your future. Meet me at the parking lot by the River Road exit at noon. We'll carpool.

Violet: Okay. But I'm over Grant, Mina. I really am. This isn't about wishing I was still with my ex. It's about not wanting to make the same mistakes I made the first time.

Mina: I hear you. And I'm going to help you make all new mistakes. I promise. Starting with getting you tipsy and facilitating your first one-afternoon-stand in a porta-potty.

Violet: Disgusting. Maybe I should stay home.

Mina: Nope. Forget about meeting me—I'll swing by and pick you up, be your designated driver so you can have a few too many and make irresponsible decisions. Be ready, leave your hair down, and wear something a little slutty. Like that backless sundress with the yellow flowers. You look gorgeous in that one.

Violet: That's Addie's, actually. And I'm pretty sure she wore it to the theme park today.

Mina: You let her out of the house in that?

Violet: She's eighteen, Mina. She leaves the house any way she wants to leave the house.

Mina: But that's a grown-woman dress and Addie is our precious baby, Violet. I refuse to believe she's not still six years old and stuffing her face with so many ham-and-feta filled apricots that she ends up throwing up in my swimming pool at least once every summer.

Violet: I know. Time has gone by so fast.

Mina: Further evidence that there is none to waste. Wear the green dress with the sequins sewn into the skirt, the one that makes you look like a mermaid, and we'll hunt you down a sexy sailor. I'll be there soon, but I'm towing the boat, so I won't be able to pull into the driveway. Meet me outside?

Violet: Be there. Ready or not, sailors here I come.

CHAPTER 4

DEACON

I need to hit the gym. Hard.

Go for an epic run.

Strap a two-hundred-pound boulder to my back and hike a thousand miles of the Pacific Coast trail.

That last option is probably my only real shot at exhausting myself enough to get Violet Boden out of my head.

I usually sleep like the dead. After years in crowded barracks as a younger man and long stints in base housing so tight you could hear your neighbors three houses down sneeze when they had a cold, I've become adept at tuning out the world in the name of a good night's rest.

But last night it was all Violet's lips and Violet's hands and the smell of her lingering on my clothes driving me out of my damned mind with wanting her. And yes, I could have changed my shirt, but then I wouldn't have been able to smell rosemary and sage with a hint of honeysuckle sweetness on top. Wouldn't have been able to close my eyes and imagine Violet riding me while I took matters into my own hand. Again. And then, just a few hours ago as the sun was rising, yet again.

The jerking off is getting embarrassing. I couldn't meet my own gaze in the mirror while I was shaving. Something has to be done. ASAP.

As soon as I pull down the drive away from the house and turn left onto the highway leading into Guerneville, I call Tristan, intending to leave a message for my unavailable baby brother—he's no doubt still shacked up in bed with his new bride—but he answers on the first ring, his voice crackling through the speakers.

"Morning, man. What's up?"

"Nothing much," I lie. Telling Tristan that I've got a chronic hard-on for one of his employees is a bad idea. "Just wondering where you were hitting the gym these days. I need to join up somewhere with enough room for interval training. The free weights in the barn aren't going to cut it much longer."

"And you're calling me? You know Rafe is the gym rat."

"But Rafe's into that Groupfit cult stuff. I can't go there. I don't like people telling me what to do."

"Don't I know it," Tristan says with a laugh. "I'm at Peak Performance by the mall right now. Going to head in later today, in fact, if you want to come along and try it out. I've got a few guest passes."

"Thanks, but I can't today. I'm working the Blues Fest—crowd control with the rest of the volunteer department." I turn right at the edge of town, heading toward River Road and a straight shot into the valley's party town. "And I thought you'd be spending the day with Zoey, soaking in newly wedded bliss."

"Oh, we're soaking in it. Even if it isn't exactly legal yet."

"Doesn't have to be legal to be real," I say, adding in a gruffer voice, "It was a really nice ceremony, Tristan. I'm glad to see you so happy. You deserve a great girl."

"Thanks, man. So do you. Given any more thought to letting Sophie set you up with one of her friends from the coffee shop?"

I grunt. "Sophie's dating Dad."

"So?"

"So her judgment is suspect."

Tristan chuckles. "Aw, Dad's not that bad. And he's been going through some kind of renaissance of the self lately. Reflecting on his actions and making changes and embracing love and forgiveness and all that."

"The hippies finally got to him, huh?" I tease, though I know Dad's always had a free-love side. He did have four sons with three different women, after all, and he only married two of his baby mamas.

"Yep," Tristan confirms. "Me, too. I've been going to an acupuncturist in Sebastopol for the knee I messed up running cross-country in college. She's changed my life. You should give her a try. She might be able to help with your shoulder."

"Thanks, but if it gets bad enough that being stabbed with needles sounds like a good idea, I'll just hurl my gimpy old body off a cliff and be done with it."

"God, you're so much like Dad. You realize this, right?"

"Nope, not even a little bit," I deny, though his words hit closer to home than I would like. Of all of my father's children, I'm the most set in my ways. There's a reason I spent twenty-five years in the military and why I'm working for a fire department now—I enjoy defined protocols and a common mission. I like a work culture that keeps emotions in check and personality quirks from turning a cut-and-dried operation into a clusterfuck.

Feelings complicate too much of life already.

Like this strong feeling I have that getting Violet out of my head is going to take more than a hardcore workout...

Still, I've got to try something.

"Maybe I can take you up on that gym offer later this week?" I ask.

"Absolutely. We could go after you check out the brush situation at the shelter."

"Sounds good, I'll be there bright and early tomorrow."

"Perfect," Tristan says. "I want to be sure we're ready for fire season next year. The smoke got way too close this time around."

I assure Tristan we'll get the shelter in wildfire-prevention shape, tell him to say hi to Zoey for me, and end the call as I tap the brakes, slowing as the taillights of the car in front of me flash red. Traffic's already backed up for miles outside of downtown Guerneville, where the Blues Fest is hosted at the Main Street river beach. Later this afternoon, the trip from one end of town to the other, a journey that usually takes no more than five minutes, will have people stuck in their cars for over an hour.

The crowds for this event get bigger and wilder every year, making extra peacekeeping staff essential. My crew of volunteer firemen will be focused mainly on cracking down on illegal fireworks and glass containers and assisting the paramedics in the first aid tent. But Chief Brolin over at the main firehouse warned that if things get too rowdy with the revelers, local law enforcement might need my team to step in with traffic control.

It's going to be a long day, but I'm looking forward to it. It's a gorgeous, cool but sunny afternoon, I like the men and women I work with, and I love the blues. If all goes well, I'll spend the afternoon being a productive member of society and the evening sipping a few beers while catching the last band's performance from my buddy's boat.

And maybe, just maybe, by the time I head home, I'll be too tired to dream about Violet Boden.

No sooner has the thought planted roots in my head than a convertible towing a tiny pontoon boat zips past me, zooming around to cut in front of my truck as we both steer into the turn lane headed down to the beach.

And right there, in the passenger's seat, with her long dark hair pulled into a ponytail and a big grin on her pretty face, is none other than the woman who's been haunting my dreams—and my dick—like the ghost of Sex-mas past.

It's almost enough to make a man start believing in things like Fate.

But if this is Fate's idea of fun, she's got one sick sense of humor.

I hang back, letting two trucks coming from the opposite direction turn into the parking lot in front of me. And when I finally swing in, I take the long way around to the staff lot, doing my best to avoid a face-to-face run-in with Ms. Boden.

But the moment I reach the help tent, where the volunteer force will be based for the day, I realize resistance is futile.

Violet's friends' boat is anchored right smack-dab in front of this stretch of beach, and Violet is already on deck, wearing a silky green dress so loose on top it shows the sexy black bikini beneath. And she's dancing. Again. With that shameless sensuality that unravels every last bit of my sanity.

And of course, I'm not the only one who's noticed. Ferris, my second-in-command, catches me gazing out across the water and hums beneath his breath. "I know, right? I wouldn't mind being tied to her bedpost with some of that hair."

"Wouldn't that get awkward?" Hoover, a newbie who's testing out the firefighter life as a volunteer before taking the test to join the main force, cocks his head to one side. "Neither of you would be able to move very much."

"Don't over think it, kid." Ferris claps him on the back with a sigh. "That one's out of your league, anyway."

"And old enough to be his damn mother," I snap, realizing my words emerged sharper than I intended when Ferris's brows shoot up and a wounded puppy look flashes on Hoover's face. "She's a friend," I add in a gentler tone. "Sort of."

Ferris's lips curve into a shit-eating grin. "Gotcha. So what is she? Ex-girlfriend?"

"Never got that far," I grumble, pretending to be very busy organizing the stack of fishing license fliers at the edge of the table. "She wasn't interested in dating."

"Ouch." Hoover nods sympathetically. "Hey, it happens. Even when you're not old."

Ferris snorts, and I find myself fighting a smile. "My advanced age wasn't the problem. It was my distasteful personality," I say dryly, earning a chuckle from Ferris.

Hoover's cheeks flush. "I don't think your personality is distasteful. You're way nicer than my grandpa."

"Your grandpa?" Ferris thunks Hoover on the back of the head. "Seriously? You need to give it a break, kid, before you dig this hole all the way to China. Deacon's only forty-five."

"Just because I live with my grandparents," Hoover says, holding his hands up in surrender. "Not because he's old as my grandpa. I didn't mean it that way."

"Don't worry about it, Hoover," I say, sliding my sunglasses into place. "I don't get my feelings hurt that easy. I'm headed toward the bridge. When Barkley and Simmons get back from their patrol, you two head down to the dam and back. Chief Brolin wanted us to make sure no kids ended up playing down there. Too many snakes, even this time of year."

"Will do, boss." Hoover gives me a little salute as I head out, and Ferris rolls his eyes, but I can tell he likes the new recruit. Ferris comes from a long line of volunteer firefighters. His twin sister, Fiona, is also part of the Russian River auxiliary department, but she had a tree-climbing competition today.

42

There's always something to do in Sonoma County in the fall, which means I should have no trouble finding a distraction from the woman presently chugging a glass of lemonade on the deck of a certain gently rocking pontoon boat. Whoever made that lemonade should hire her to star in their commercials. The look on her face as her throat works in the afternoon sun is enough to make me thicker.

Damn, that must be some really good lemonade.

She looks almost as happy as she did on Halloween night when I was—

Don't think about it, asshole. Think about boiled cabbage, paper cuts on your tongue, the smell of the fishmonger's garbage by that bar in Korea.

Memories of the nightmare stink lingering outside that fish stall on my last deployment are about to steer my thoughts out of the lust zone and back to the job at hand, when a chorus of honking echoes through the air, loud enough to give the guitar solo a run for its money.

I glance up to see a flock of geese soaring low, no doubt coming to check out the picnic scraps blown off blankets by the increasingly serious wind. I watch them for a beat, admiring the elegant curves of their wings and long, feathered necks before starting down the beach, keeping an eye out for contraband I've been authorized to seize and destroy.

I've barely made it five steps when the music is pierced by a sharp *pop pop pop*, followed by an animal wail of distress and a sudden burst of cheering from a group of kids near the roped-off swimming area. In my peripheral vision, I see one of the geese drop from the sky, plummeting toward the water with one wing thrust out awkwardly to the side. A quick scan of the shore reveals a red-haired boy with a missing front tooth thrusting a BB gun into the air, while the kids surrounding him—mostly boys and mostly locals judging by the looks of their tattered swim shorts—slap him on the back and pump fists in the air.

It's a scene straight out of *Lord of the Flies*, lawlessness without a voice of parental reason in sight.

A frown pulling at my forehead, I start toward the group. Weapons of any kind, even BB guns, are forbidden on public beaches. I'm going to have to confiscate the weapon and probably run this entire crew off the beach. I seriously doubt they have tickets to the festival, and the beach isn't open to the general public today.

I'm about to give the entire rabble a talking to in my Mean Dad voice, the one Jacob and Blake assure me scared the shit out of them until they were at least thirteen or fourteen, when a woman cries out, "No, Violet! Don't! The current is too strong."

I turn to see Violet—who clearly doesn't listen to *anyone's* good advice—diving into the water not far from where the wounded goose is honking and flapping a few meters away.

Her head goes under, and I curse, but I'm not too worried. Surely she can swim, or she wouldn't have jumped in.

Surely...

I count to ten, then to twenty. By thirty I'm shucking my jacket and running for the shoreline. I kick off my shoes, heart racing as the numbers climb higher—thirty-eight, thirty-nine, forty—with no sign of Violet. She must have hit her head or gotten tangled up in something under the water.

Grabbing one of the red emergency flotation devices hanging from the empty lifeguard stand—I'm going to strangle that kid when he gets back from the bathroom or the beer tent or wherever he's gone—I rush into the water, swimming hard for the place where I saw Violet's head go under.

CHAPTER 5

VIOLET

I plunge beneath the surface of the rocking waves, screaming with my mouth closed as every cell in my body howls in protest to the sudden, frigid assault.

Son of Zeus, it's fucking freezing!

My head swims, and my shocked arms stiffen in the water, not sure what to do with themselves. For a moment, I can't remember where I am, *who* I am, my mental slate wiped clean by the trauma of going from sun-warm on a boat deck to submerged in frosty, early November river water.

I sink fast, plunging through the increasingly murky depths until I hit bottom. The moment my toes squish into the soft sand and gravel of the riverbed, my thoughts jolt back into motion.

Move, Violet. Swim! Up to the surface. Swim. Fast. Now!

I push off the bottom, pulling hard through the water toward the surface with my half-numb arms, my heart thudding fast as I realize how little air is left in my lungs and how far I've managed to sink beneath the surface.

I refuse to die like this, to leave my girls alone in the world to fend for themselves because I underestimated Mother Nature. I should have known better. It's still warm during the day, but the nighttime temperatures have been getting down to the low forties, probably even lower here in the river valley.

As I break the surface, pulling in a deep lungful of air, I silently vow never to set foot on a boat after Labor Day. I will save that goose, get to shore, and stay there until summer comes back around next year.

"Violet! Oh my God, are you okay?" Mina shouts from the boat behind me.

I wave at my frantic-looking friend and call out, "Fine. I'm fine."

Mina's caramel curls bounce as she races across the deck. "I'm going to throw you the flamingo floatie!"

"I don't need it, it's fine," I insist, knowing the giant pink inner tube will only make it more difficult to maneuver through the choppy water.

Shivering hard, I shove my hair out of my eyes and scan the waves around me, almost immediately spotting the struggling bird. Its wide eyes and panicked honking resonate with me in a major way.

"I hear you, m-mama," I say, pulling toward her. "I'm coming. Don't worry."

I'm trying to figure out the best way to tow her back to shore without getting pecked to death in the process —she won't know I'm trying to help her, the poor thing, and will probably put up a decent fight, despite her wounded wing—when I'm suddenly snatched from behind.

A massive arm latches around my waist, pulling me against a warm, lightly furred chest and a puffy red life preserver that bonks me solidly on the head.

"Wait, I'm okay! We n-need to help her," I say, teeth chattering so hard I can barely hear myself over the music throbbing across the water. Seems I'm the only person who thought a wounded goose was reason enough to stop the party.

"You were under the water for almost a minute. You're going straight to the first aid tent," comes a familiar voice so close to my ear I can feel his lips moving against my damp skin.

His full, warm lips…

By some mad twist of fate, it's Deacon. Deacon's arm around my waist and Deacon's hand oh-so-close to my breast and Deacon's legs tangling with mine as we tread water in the increasingly rocky waves.

And just like that, I'm on fire. Still freezing, yes, but I'm also burning, aching, my blood turning to lava as the urge to rub against Deacon like a cat in heat returns with a vengeance.

I make a silent note to make a doctor's appointment first thing tomorrow—surely there has to be something medically wrong with me that I'm dying to hump a man's leg while in danger of hypothermia—and shove lust away into a dark mental corner where it belongs.

"I'm fine. Really. But she's not." I jab a finger toward the goose. The current is picking up, too, dragging the struggling animal downstream. "We have to at least try to help her."

Breath rushing out, warm and sweet against my neck, Deacon says, "I'll take you in first and come back for her."

"There's no time, she'll be too far away by then. We have to go now." I try to paddle closer, but Deacon has me locked up tight. He's huge. Even bigger and stronger than my ex. There's no way I'm going to be able to physically overpower him. My only chance is to appeal to his softer side—assuming he has one.

I glance over my shoulder at him, breath catching as our eyes meet.

He looks so worried. Almost…scared. For me.

On instinct, I reach up, laying a hand on his cheek. "I'm fine," I assure him again, holding his troubled gaze. "I promise."

"You shouldn't have jumped in. A bird isn't worth risking your life."

"She's a creature in pain," I say, willing him to understand. "I can't stand by and watch another living thing suffer. Not if there's a chance I can help."

"People eat geese," he snaps.

"I don't. I'm a vegan. But if I did, I would eat a goose that had been humanely raised and slaughtered, not one who'd been injured and doomed to a slow painful death by drowning or infection or being chomped on by coyotes because she's too injured to fly away." I cast a quick glance across the water, heart leaping as I see the bird beginning to sink lower as she's dragged away. Turning back to Deacon, I funnel every ounce of passion in my shivering body into my words. "Would you want to die like that? Scared and alone and hurting and not even knowing why? She won't understand what

49

happened to her, Deacon, but I do. And I know that animal doesn't deserve to go out that way."

His brow furrows and his jaw locks tight, but after a beat he sighs again—an exasperated sound that makes it clear I'm the most frustrating person he's ever had the misfortune to attempt to save—and nods sharply. "Fine. Two minutes. If we don't have her by then, we're going in and you're not giving me any more shit about it."

A smile curving my trembling lips, I nod. "Deal."

Deacon shifts the long red flotation device, tucking it under both of our arms until we're side-by-side in the water. I kick hard, but it soon becomes clear that I probably don't need to bother. Deacon's churning legs carry us across the surface at fighter-pilot speed, closing in on our little girl so fast I don't have time to get nervous about how the actual rescue is going to go down. One moment we're surging through the waves and the next I'm gripping the back of the wounded bird's neck firmly in one hand while cradling her body against the squishy red rubber of the floatie with the other.

She thrashes once, letting out a pitiful honk, but quickly goes still as Deacon turns us around and starts back toward shore.

"I think she's in shock," I whisper, not wanting to upset her even more. "We'll need to get her to the vet right away. We have a wild animal guy on call at the shelter, but it will take at least an hour to get to Healds-burg in this traffic. Think there's anyone closer?"

"There's a vet here in town," Deacon says. "She's not open on Sundays, but she'll come in for an emergency. I'll get one of the other volunteers to run the bird over there as soon as we're on shore."

"I can do it. Just tell me the address and—"

"No. You're going to the first aid tent to get checked out."

My eyebrows snap together, and the hairs on the back of my neck prickle to attention. "I'd rather go with her. She's calm with me. It's important not to put her through any more stress than absolutely necessary."

"And it's important you don't get hypothermia. I mean, assuming you care about being there when your daughter gets home tonight."

"Of course I care," I snap, but softly, so as not to upset my patient. "For your information, I'm an excellent parent."

He grunts, and my blood pressure rises a few more degrees.

"What's that supposed to mean? That grunt?"

"It means that from where I'm sitting, your priorities are out of order."

My clenched jaw drops, but before I can ask him where he gets off judging my priorities or anything else, my feet touch bottom, and I'm too busy scrambling onto shore to bother. My dress clings to my legs, making me fight for every step as I stumble across the gravel, carrying the bird into the waiting arms of a man in a Russian River Volunteer Fire Department T-shirt who's holding a gray blanket I hope my patient will find comforting.

"We've already called Sarah at the animal hospital," the man tells Deacon, cradling the goose against his broad chest with a tenderness that makes me feel better about trusting her in a stranger's hands. "She's going to meet us there in a few minutes."

"Good." Deacon's fingers close around my upper arm, sending twin flashes of annoyance and awareness sizzling across my chilled skin. "I'm going to escort Violet to the first aid tent. Tell Ferris to take point until I get back, and have Hoover put a call into the firehouse, let them know we may need reinforcements if we lose any more staff."

The man nods. "Got it, boss."

He turns, carrying the goose away, and my heart does a sad flip in my chest. A part of me wants to hurry after him, stay right by that wounded creature's side until she's nursed back to health, and then take her home to live happily ever after. But my house is over-flowing with animals already, she'll be better off in the wild, and I apparently have a bossy-jerk-mandated appointment with the first aid tent.

"Come on, let's get you checked out," Deacon says, his voice gruff.

"I can find my way on my own," I say, squirming my arm free. "Wouldn't want to inconvenience you."

"You've already inconvenienced me, and I'm soaked. I need to dry off, and they've got towels in the tent." He glances down at my dress. "You should probably get out of those wet clothes, too."

And that's all it takes—just the mention of getting out of my clothes from the lips of this frustrating, rage-stroke-inducing man—and my already-hard nipples pull even tighter. Electricity dances across my skin, and heat rushes up my neck, and it's suddenly all I can do not to wrap my arms around Deacon's shoulders and drag his mouth down to mine.

I want to kiss him hard, so hard and deep that he won't have any breath left to boss me around. I want to show him with my lips, teeth, and tongue just how much I can't stand him. I want to rip off my wet clothes, get skin to skin with every irritating inch of him, and ride him until the urge to strangle him fades away in the supernova of pleasure that rips through my body every time he puts his hands on it.

Those presumptuous hands that are, even now, settling on my waist, lifting me up onto the boardwalk like I weigh less than the goose I just handed over.

"Get moving." He nods toward the parking lot and the festival tents beyond. "The sooner we get this done, the sooner we can go our separate ways."

"Good." I lift my chin. "Because I, for one, don't like having murderous thoughts about people. I'm a pacifist."

His lips quirk, and his blue eyes do a flashing, sparkling thing that makes my knees weak.

"What's that supposed to mean?" I ask.

He shakes his head. "What?"

I motion toward his maddening—and gorgeous—face. "That look."

"I was just thinking you're awfully confrontational for a pacifist."

"I am not," I snap, nose scrunching when his brows curve into a "see what I mean?" squiggle. "Fine." I sigh. "You could have a point. A small point. I'll go to the first aid tent without a fight, but I would like my reluctance to be noted."

"Noted," he says with another smug grin I'd like to slap off his face.

But that wouldn't be very peace-loving, either. So I don't.

I follow him to the first aid area with my arms crossed over my chest, keeping my hands, and my traitorous nipples, to myself.

CHAPTER 6

DEACON

*O*ne look at the pair of us, soaked to the skin and shivering in the cool wind, and the two nurses at the first aid tent leap into action.

"Oh, you poor things, did you fall overboard?" The female nurse with curly red hair bustles Violet behind a privacy partition on one side of the tent without waiting for an answer. "Don't worry, we'll get you all fixed up and dried out. There should be a stack of towels back there. Wrap up in one, give me your dress, and I'll pop up to the main lodge and throw it into the dryer."

"Thank you so much," Violet says.

She continues to speak—something about the goose and the animal hospital—that I lose track of as I'm bustled through the tent's back exit by the second nurse. We emerge into a private grassy area surrounded by trees, where several lawn chairs are arranged in front of a clothesline strung with beach towels.

"I can take your clothes up to the dryer, too, if you want." He grins as he brushes a hand back and forth over his tightly curled hair—also red, making me wonder if he and the other nurse are related. "Or you can hang your clothes on the line and chill out in your boxers back here." He nods toward the chairs with a wink. "I'll make sure no one bothers you. Except maybe me, when I get off my shift in an hour."

"Thanks," I say, with an only slightly uncomfortable laugh. After growing up next door to one of the hottest LGBTQ vacation spots in the country, you'd think I'd be used to getting hit on by other guys by now. And I am. Mostly. "But I'm on duty. And I've got another shirt in my truck. I will use your line, though, if that's all right. I can hang up my wet shirt and come get it later."

"Totally. Whatever you want, doll." He nods over his shoulder. "I'm Kip, by the way. I'm heading up to the main lodge with Melody to grab some more water bottles. Make yourself at home, and if anyone comes looking for us, tell them we'll be back in the shake of a lamb's tail, okay?"

"Got it," I say, turning my back as he ducks into the tent. I strip off my shirt, feeling better almost instantly. Wet jeans aren't enjoyable by any stretch, but I really can't stand the feel of a wet T-shirt clinging to me like a second skin.

I'm about to hang it on the line, when a soft sound behind me makes me glance over my shoulder to see Violet standing barefoot in the grass, wearing nothing but a rainbow-colored beach towel wrapped around her tempting little body.

Her gaze drags slowly from my hips to my chest with a weight I can almost feel. Her fingers tighten on the fabric clutched around her chest, and her toes curl into the grass, and the last of my irritation evaporates in a rush of lust so intense my hands tremble as I toss my T-shirt onto the clothesline.

Half the time, this woman drives me up the wall.

But the other half...

"I, um... I..." She trails off with a gentle shake of her head. "I forgot what I came out here to say."

The other half, she makes me want her with an intensity that's flat-out crazy, dangerous, and ill-fuck-ing-advised.

I value boundaries, logic, and level-headed interpersonal interactions. It's one of the reasons I've never done drugs and rarely drink to excess—I don't like being out of control. But one look at Violet Boden and I'm a junkie prepared to do whatever it takes to get his fix.

If I knew what's good for me, I'd head back into the tent, grab a towel, and get out of here before I do something I'll regret. Violet isn't interested. She's made that clear on numerous occasions. Continuing to pursue her is an exercise in futility and embarrassment—neither of which I enjoy.

Too bad that doesn't stop me from eating up the distance between us, wrapping my arm around Violet's waist, and pulling her close.

Her breath rushes out as her hands settle on my bare chest, but she doesn't push me away. Her fingers curl against my skin as she bites down on her bottom lip with a hungry moan that goes straight to my already aching balls. Before I know what I'm doing, my hand is fisted in her damp hair and my lips are devouring hers.

And from the first taste of her—of her absolute sweetness—I'm desperate for more. Ravenous. Starved for her touch and her breath warm on my skin and her pleasure washing over me in thick, sticky waves that make me desperate to take her. To show her how good it's going to feel when we stop fucking with words and make touch our primary mode of communication.

I don't need words. All I need are her nails digging into my shoulders and her hips arching closer to my cock and those breathy sounds she makes that let me know I'm doing everything right.

"We have to stop," she pants against my lips, even as her fingers dive into my hair, pulling me closer still.

"I don't want to stop. I want my tongue between your legs," I say, groaning as she shudders against me and her leg skims up to wrap around my thigh. "I'm off at four. We'll go to my place. I'll make you dinner."

"I don't want dinner." Her head falls back, and I devour her neck, biting and kissing as her grip tightens in my hair. "I don't need food."

"Me, either. All I need is your body." My heart jerks hard in my chest, threatening to stop beating as she rocks her hips forward, rubbing against my erection through my damp jeans. "God, Violet, I want to be inside you so fucking much. I want to take you right here on the grass."

"Yes." She sucks in a breath as I reach between the folds of her towel, finding the soft curls between her legs and gliding two fingers inside where she's already so slick and hot. "Now. Yes. Please. Inside me."

"We can't," I say, the logical side of my brain shouting to be heard over the lust monster breathing fire into my veins.

"It's private back here," she says. "No one will see."

"Kip and Melody will be back any minute."

"Then we'd better hurry." Violet reaches for the close of my jeans, but I catch her fingers, stopping her before she can pull my cock out in public at an event where I'm supposed to be organizing ten other volunteer firefighters.

But a part of me doesn't want to stop her.

A part of me wants to roll Violet down to the ground, unwrap her like the best Christmas present ever, and fuck her on the grass in plain view of Kip or anyone else who decides to step through to the back of the first aid tent. I want her that much, that desperately, that insanely.

It's *insane*, what she does to me. Truly fucking crazy.

"Woah. Hold up." I step back, lifting my arms into the air at my sides in surrender.

But this doesn't feel like giving in, it feels like begging for mercy, for strength, for the real Deacon to show the hell up and keep junkie Deacon from making a career-and-reputation killing mistake. I'm at the top of the list for the next Volunteer Fire Chief, one of the only paid positions in the volunteer department. But I'm sure that would change if I were caught in flagrante delicto with the drowning victim I just pulled out of the river.

And I want that job. Badly.

I want to feel useful again, to stop filling my days as an unpaid hired hand on my father's farm and wishing I'd been able to retire from the Air Force two years earlier, when my boys were still at home. Before they went off to college and left me feeling like a boring, used up old fogey too hopelessly out of touch to be of any interest to the kids who have been my reason for living for so long.

Putting that at risk to get my rocks off would be as stupid as jumping into freezing water to save a bird most people would gladly eat for dinner.

"This can't happen," I say, taking another step back. "Seriously."

"Fine." Violet crosses her arms over her chest, tucking the towel more firmly around that body I'm dying to have bared to me again.

Just not here. Or now.

I'm about to suggest we meet by my truck at four, when I'll be free to whisk her away to a more suitable location, when Violet jerks her chin higher. "If you'll remember, I'm the one who tried to stop first." She motions between us. "Because *this* can't happen. Like I said last night, we aren't a good fit."

"And like I said, you barely know me." I prop my hands low on my hips, digging my fingers into damp jean fabric instead of Violet's addictive skin. "I mean, clearly there's chemistry here."

She blinks faster, but her nose stays firmly in the air. "Chemistry isn't enough to sustain a relationship, and I'm not into random hookups."

I arch a brow, and irritation flickers across her features.

"Okay. Fine. Yes." She wiggles her fingers at the ground. "So I was up for banging in the grass a few minutes ago, but that's just further proof that we're a bad idea. I'm not usually like this. I usually make reasonable decisions."

My lips part, but before I can speak, she rushes on.

"And yes, jumping into the river to save that goose was a reasonable decision. One I would make again. Because life is precious and worth defending. But this…" She eases back a step until her shoulders brush the towel hung on the line behind her. "This is a waste of your time. And mine."

Stung more than I would like to admit, I clench my jaw and nod stiffly. "Then I guess I won't be seeing you around."

She swallows. "I guess not."

"Fine," I say.

"Fine," she echoes.

And it is fine. Just fucking fine.

So why do I still want to kiss her so badly that my hand is shaking as I snatch my shirt from the line and head for the exit, leaving the first aid tent—and Violet Boden—far behind.

CHAPTER 7

From the texts of Violet Boden
and Mina Smalls

Mina: Just checking to make sure you got home okay. I hate that you took a car service without asking me to drive you first. I wouldn't have minded at all. Anyway, now I'm worried you were kidnapped by a rogue Uber driver. Text me, okay?

Violet: Sorry! Didn't mean to worry you. I got home and got busy feeding the animals and forgot to text. But yes, I'm fine, everything's fine.

Mina: You didn't seem fine when you called before. You seemed upset.

Violet: No, just...rattled, I guess.

Mina: Well, who can blame you?! You almost drowned!

Violet: I did not almost drown. I was fine.

Mina: You were under the water an awfully long time, Vi. I know I was happy to see a gorgeous firefighter swimming to your rescue.

Violet: But I didn't need rescuing. Especially by Deacon Jerkface Hunter.

Mina: What? Why? What did he do? OMG, he didn't cop a feel or something while he was saving you, did he? Leave it to a man to be dumb enough to ruin heroism by getting handsy.

Violet: No, nothing like that. He's just a jerk. A steaming hot, bossy jerk. I swear, he makes me want to claw his eyes out, and I never feel that way. About anyone. But something about him sets my teeth on edge. He's like the human equivalent of nails on a chalk-board. Or bubblegum in your hair. Or gnats in your lemonade.

Mina: OMG. He's the one! He's the guy!

Violet: What guy?

Mina: The one who Sleeping Beautied your vagina!

Violet: Sigh...

Mina: Ha!! I knew it! He's the guy who's been driving you crazy, and he jumped into a freezing river to save you! Oh, Violet, it's so romantic!

Violet: It is not romantic. I didn't need saving!

Mina: Okay, fine, so you didn't need saving. But he didn't know that. He saw you go under and leaped to the rescue. I think it's lovely. Most of the men I've dated in the past year wouldn't jump into a hot tub to save me, let alone a freezing cold river with a rushing current and a dangerously pissed-off goose on the loose.

Violet: The goose wasn't dangerous. She was so sweet. Didn't give me a bit of trouble on the way to shore. I hope she's all right. I tried to call the vet in Guerneville to check on her, but they didn't answer.

Mina: Don't try to change the subject. I don't want to talk about waterfowl. I want to talk about when you're meeting up with the big sexy firefighter for a twenty-four-hour sex-a-thon.

Violet: Never! He's awful. Are you even reading these texts?

Mina: I'm reading between the lines, sugar, and what I'm seeing is lust. Lots of hot, sticky, rampaging, unsatisfied lust. And the longer you delay the inevitable, the crankier you're going to get.

Violet: I am not cranky! ARGH!

Mina: *skeptical eyebrows emoji*

Violet: Okay, so I'm cranky, but not because of Deacon Hunter. Pansy threw up in my running shoes again while I was gone, and I just spent twenty minutes cleaning cat vomit off of my hundred dollar arch supports.

Mina: I'm sorry about that. And that your ancient cat has an anxiety disorder. But again, I must insist we stay focused on more interesting topics. Deacon is the perfect guy for this stage in your life, Violet! You're not looking for love or big emotional upheaval. You've had enough of that in your marriage. What you need is a fine-assed man with a functional dick who knows his way around a pussy.

Violet: Must you be so crass about it?

Mina: Yes, I must. We're too old to be coy, sister. And you're the one who told me to fuck, fuck, fuck until I ran out of dicks.

Violet: No, I didn't, LOL!

Mina: Well, someone smart said that. Oh, it was Gabrielle Union! In her memoir. Anyway, it's so true. You're in the prime of your life, and so is that gorgeous poose of yours. It's a tragedy that you've kept her under lock and key for so long. Set a date for dong with Deacon.

Violet: Again, I'll remind you that I can't stand him.

Mina: All the better! That way you know you won't get in too deep. The rebound danger is real with your first guy post divorce, Vi. You don't want to get emotionally attached just because you're naked with someone new for the first time. Yes, naked used to mean making love to a person who cared about you. But now naked just means naked. Best to go in a little pissed off at your new boy toy. It'll help keep your head on straight.

Violet: That sounds so...depressing.

Mina: It's not. I promise. There's great fun to be had in the dating jungle as long as you don't take any of it too seriously. And it's great that he's older. He might actually be able to last longer than five minutes the first few times. I adore my hot babies, don't get me wrong, but there are definite advantages to having a full-grown man in your bed.

Violet: He's certainly full-grown...

Mina: Oh yeah? Do tell? Is he hung like a sperm whale?

Violet: More like a banana slug. They're hermaphrodites with penises as long as their entire bodies. Also, they occasionally bite them off their partner when they're finished mating. True fact.

Mina: Repulsive. I'm so glad you work at an animal shelter and learn such horrific things to share with me.

Violet: It's Zoey's fault. She has a way with gross animal

facts. They get stuck in my head and I can't get them out.

Mina: Right. That reminds me, we should have a talk before you and Mr. Well Hung get down to business. Make sure you're prepared for the big event. Pun intended.

Violet: Ha. Thanks, but no thanks. I'm not going to call him, Mina. It just doesn't feel right. If I'm going to be intimate with someone, I want it to be a person I have more in common with than chemistry, no matter how combustible it is.

Mina: All right. Fine. Maybe I'll swipe right on that bad boy. See what all the fuss is about.

Violet: Swipe him and die, woman.

Mina: LOL! See, I knew you liked him!

Violet: Grrr... I do not. And he isn't online anyway. He thinks online dating is dumb and that I'm dumb, and I'm sure he's fine with never seeing me again.

Mina: Negative. It's only a matter of time, Violet. You can fight it all you want, but sooner or later something's going to happen between you and Deacon. I can feel it. My IUD is tingling.

Violet: I prefer to have my fortune read in tea leaves, thank you.

Mina: Joke all you want, but my birth control knows. It always knows…

Violet: Goodbye, Mina. I've got more cat vomit to clean.

Mina: Goodbye, my little sex kitten. Hope you get some sleep tonight…

CHAPTER 8

VIOLET

*C*ursed...

I've been cursed...that's what's happening here.

A part of me wants to blame Mina for jinxing my sleep with her text yesterday, or Adriana for not getting home until almost midnight on a school night, forcing me to yell at her like a responsible parent before sending her up to bed, but I know who's really to blame.

Deacon Hunter and the hex he's put on my sex drive. He doesn't look like the kind of guy who practices the dark arts, but it's always the ones you least expect. He's probably holed up in a creepy witch doctor shed right now, sticking pins in a voodoo vagina stuffed with strands of my hair and plotting all the ways he's going to shatter my resistance to his banana-slug penis.

Only it's nothing like a banana slug. It's not gross or slimy. From the feel I copped down the front of his pants the night of the party, I know it's long and thick with a sweetly plump head, and that I want to kiss it almost as much as I want to kiss the man it belongs to. I want to return the oral favor he so generously bestowed upon me so much it makes my mouth water every time I think about it.

I'm dying to give a man a blowjob. I can't remember the last time that happened—if it's ever happened at all.

"Black magic," I grumble as I throw leftover tuna fish salad and crackers in Addie's lunch box. "It's the only answer."

"Mom have you seen my water bottle?" she calls from the top of the stairs. "It's not in my backpack."

Scanning the kitchen countertops, I spot Addie's purse and her massive, sticker-covered water bottle sticking out of one side. "Yeah. I see it. I'll rinse it out for you. But you need to hurry, Adriana, I have to be at a meeting in twenty minutes. I don't have time to drive you if you miss the bus."

A beleaguered, "I know, Mom. Please and thank you," drifts down the stairs in response, making me roll my eyes.

"If you know, then why do you miss the bus at least twice a week?" I mutter to myself as I grab the water bottle, sending a sheet of notebook paper inside Addie's purse fluttering to the floor in the process.

I bend down, grabbing the page, intending to stuff it back in with the rest of the mess and move on to water-bottle rinsing—not to read it or to invade my daughter's privacy; I'm not that kind of mom, never have been—when I see it.

That four-letter word...

Love you. Drive safe and text me when you get home. Had a

blast with you this weekend and can't wait to see you again, sexy. Xo, Jacob

By the time I'm done reading, my eyes are about to bulge out of my head. What the fresh hell is this? As far as I know, Adriana isn't even *dating* anyone seriously, let alone *in love* with some kid who calls her "sexy."

Oh God…

Sexy…

It's happening. Again. My last virgin daughter is about to have a close encounter with a penis. Heck, judging by the tone of this little love note, she may have *already* had a close encounter with a penis. She hasn't asked me to make her an appointment to get birth control sorted out, the way she swore she would when she was ready to take that next step, but that doesn't mean she's not sexually active.

Adriana is all about breaking her promises lately.

And lying to her parents like it's her job. This note is hard evidence that she didn't spend the weekend at Six Flags with her girlfriends the way she said she did. She spent it with a boy doing God only knows what and who knows where.

Thankfully, she made it home safely last night, but if she hadn't, I would have had no idea where to tell the police to start looking for her. I didn't know who she was really with or where she was going. This Jacob person could have killed my baby, buried her in an abandoned mine shaft somewhere outside of Sacramento, and walked away without ever being forced to pay for his crimes—all because Adriana decided to go through a sneaky phase before heading off to college.

The protective mama bear inside me wants to storm

up the stairs, confront Adriana with the note, and ground her for the rest of her natural life.

Instead, I tuck the scrap of paper back into her purse and cross to the sink to rinse out the water bottle. Addie is eighteen. In seven months, she'll be leaving to work as a counselor at a track and field summer camp and then heading to Cal Poly to start her freshman year.

She's slipping through my fingers, so close to gone that I have to play this carefully. Yes, she's still living under my roof for a few more months, but if I want to continue to have any influence over her behavior in the long term, I have to get to the bottom of what's behind this rebellious phase, gather her back into the trust fold, and make her think it was her idea to start telling her mother her secrets again.

So even though I'm dying to shove a box of condoms into her bag and remind her that we Boden women are excessively fertile—which is why she needs a backup form of birth control in place at all times—I bite my tongue. And when she hurries down the stairs in jean overalls and braids, looking way too young to be having sex, I simply hand over her water bottle and kiss her cheek.

"Are we doing dinner? Or do you have late practice again this week?" I ask, grabbing my purse and keys and following her out of the kitchen.

"Late practice, so I'll just grab a sandwich out," she says, snagging her jacket from the hook by the front door. "But I should be back by eight if you want to watch a movie or something."

"I'd love to watch a movie. I'll have popcorn ready when you get home."

Addie smiles at me over her shoulder. "Thanks, Mom. You're the best. Love you."

"Love you, too," I say, heart twisting as I watch her bound down the porch steps and jog to the end of the block where her friends from the neighborhood are already waiting for the bus. And for a moment, I don't see her as she is, but as she was, that giggling, wide-eyed, bundle of energy I sent off to kindergarten for the first time thirteen years ago with a Pokemon lunch box and a ponytail in the middle of her forehead she called her unicorn horn.

She's still my baby, and she always will be. And if necessary, I will hunt down this kid who's so eager to get his mitts all over my little girl, put that box full of condoms directly into his hands, and promise to personally cut off his nuts if he doesn't use them properly.

But hopefully, that won't be necessary. I just need to figure out what made Addie start pulling away from her dad and me in the first place, yank that weed out by the root, and get our love garden back in tip-top shape.

Which, unfortunately, involves talking to my ex for longer than five minutes. I slide into my Prius with a sigh, punching the power button and rolling out into the early morning downtown Santa Rosa traffic.

We've had this coffee date scheduled for over a week. Grant wants to discuss Addie's dipping grades—he thinks a B-plus in Calculus is reason for alarm—and I want to discuss the missing hours between Addie leaving my house and showing up at his for her weekend visits.

Now, however, I'm pretty sure I know what she's been up to when she disappeared.

The question is…do I share it with Grant? I pull into Nitro Joe's a few blocks away from the Big Bad Bank where he works, debating the pros and cons of telling my infamously unreasonable ex that his baby girl has a secret lover, and find Grant already sitting at a table in the front garden.

He's early, something that hasn't happened in….

Ever?

Grant is always late. Chronic tardiness is ingrained in his DNA, a trait sadly passed on to two of our three daughters. But here he is, dressed in one of his eight hundred dollar suits, with his silver and black hair perfectly swooped up in front, and two lattes on pale blue saucers on the café table in front of him. He's even grabbed one of the sugar bowls with cubes in it that I like, instead of the packets of diet poison sweetener he prefers.

Something is definitely up…

My ex-drama sensors are blaring out a Code Red warning—lifting all the hairs on my arms as I step out of the car into the cool breeze—when my phone starts barking in my purse, signaling a Code Red of another kind. It's Virginia's ringtone, and she never calls this early unless there's trouble at the shelter.

Lifting a hand with an I-have-to-take-this finger raised to Grant, I bring my cell to my ear, "Hey, Ginny, what's up?"

"Violet you have to come quick! They're after our salamanders!"

I squint into the morning sun, my yet-to-be-caffeinated brain struggling for a moment before I remember the little guys we discovered living in some

74

abandoned ground squirrel burrows behind the shelter last winter. Virginia is a big amphibian fan, in general, but the beauties in our backyard are endangered California tiger salamanders, a fact that made the discovery even more thrilling.

But now, apparently, someone is "after them?"

"They're going to rip all the shrubs out and kill them, Violet," Virginia continues before I can ask who is after our 'manders and why. "They can't survive without groundcover. They'll get too hot in the summer, and their burrows will flood and collapse in the winter. We have to do something, but I know they won't listen to me."

"Who, Virginia? Who won't listen to you?" I ask, plugging my other ear in an attempt to hear her better over the roar of early morning traffic on College Avenue. "Is Tristan there? Can you get him to intervene? Or Zoey?"

"Zoey's out on a food run, and Tristan is part of the problem." Virginia makes a pitiful whimpering sound that makes me wish I was there to give her a hug. Ginny can be a prickly pear when you first meet her, but underneath the bluster, she's all heart. "Please, Violet. I'll stall them with coffee, but you've got to get here before he goes for the bulldozer. Hurry!"

"Bulldozer?" I frown-blink. "What on earth—"

I'm cut off by a scuffing sound on the other end of the line as Virginia hangs up. I sigh, the arm holding my phone dropping to my side.

So it's going to be one of those Mondays. Lovely.

I lift an arm to Grant as he pushes through the

wrought iron gate surrounding the outdoor seating and says, "Hey. You should sit. The coffee's getting cold."

I shake my head. "I'm sorry. I can't stay, after all. There's an emergency at work. Virginia's freaking out, says I need to get there right away."

"Can't someone else handle it?" Grant asks, fingers tapping nervously on my ancient Prius's hood, near the patch of missing paint I know must be driving him crazy. "I need to talk to you."

"I know. And I know you're worried about Addie, but I really have to go. If I don't, endangered salamanders could lose their habitat."

Grant arches a brow. "Seriously?"

I nod. "Seriously."

He sighs, clearly not thrilled, but not wanting lost amphibian lives on his conscience, either. Grant might not always treat people the way I'd prefer, but he's an animal lover from way back. He never put up a fuss about adding another critter to our family, no matter how many battered creatures the girls just had to rescue.

"All right," he says, rubbing at the back of his neck. "But we need to talk soon. Not just about Addie. There's...other stuff, too."

I turn my head, studying him from the corner of my eye as fear whispers through my thoughts. Grant is in incredible physical shape, but he is getting to the age when scary things can start to go wrong. "What other stuff? Are you okay?"

"I'm fine," he says, banishing my cancer and infected hair plug fears. "I'm just..." He shakes his head, apparently at a loss for words for the first time in his life.

"Some things are happening, things I'm not sure I can walk back now that they've started and I... " He stretches his head to one side. "Maybe I haven't thought everything through the way I should have the past few years, Violet. Maybe I've taken a hard right when I should have stayed the course. You know what I mean?"

"Um, not really." I toss my purse back into the passenger's seat, secretly grateful for an excuse to jet. Whatever's got Grant worked up it sounds personal—which isn't my business anymore. "But I've really got to go, Grant. I'll text you about Addie later. I'm sure, between the two of us, we can get her back on the right track."

He sighs, his fingers curling into a fist. "Fine. But tell her I expect to see her daily quiz scores up this week. I'm checking her grades online. She's not going to graduate top of her engineering class at Cal Poly if she goes in with a soft foundation in Calculus."

I give him a thumbs-up—even though I'm not the least bit worried about my brilliant daughter's math foundation—and sink back behind the wheel. "Talk to you later."

Hopefully much later, I think as I pull out of the parking space. I have enough drama in my life right now. I don't need Grant plopping his mess on top of the pile. That's the only good thing about suddenly becoming a single parent so late in life, I'm no longer responsible for helping my disaster-prone husband out of the messes he somehow always managed to find his way into.

Now, it's my problems and the girls' problems —that's it.

Well, and Virginia's problems. At least, this morning.

I swing into the shelter's parking lot twenty minutes later to find Ginny waiting for me at the end of the walk leading up to the shelter, pacing back and forth, rattling the wooden bracelets on her wrist like a witchdoctor warding away evil. The moment she sees me, she hustles across the pavement, urgently motioning for me to hurry.

"They're finalizing the plans," she says, nervous energy vibrating off of her in waves. "You have to go. Now. Run. I'll catch up."

She grabs my purse and lunchbox from me, tucking them both under one arm as she puts a hand between my shoulder blades and shoves—none too gently. And even though I seriously doubt this situation is urgent enough to require a sprint up to the office building, I take off, jogging through the cool morning. I'd rather run and feel silly than walk and upset Virginia any more than she is already.

I'm mentally composing what I'm going to say to my boss—how to explain to Tristan that endangered salamander lives are in his hands—when the front door opens and the man himself steps out into the sunshine, with six feet two inches of trouble right behind him.

It's Deacon. Again.

Looking even sexier in the flesh than he did in all my dirty dreams last night.

CHAPTER 9

DEACON

*V*iolet stumbles to a stop in front of me, her eyes going wide and her lips parting in a soft O that immediately makes me think of things I shouldn't. Things like the dream that woke me up in a sweat this morning, featuring Miss Boden wearing nothing but a pair of tiny lace panties and a hungry look on her pretty face.

But I refuse to get a hard-on in front of my kid brother.

Or Violet.

I'm done with this woman. I don't care how hot the chemistry is between us. I've got a high tolerance for pain, but I'm not a glutton for punishment.

"Hey, Violet, what's up?" Tristan asks, glancing past her to the twitchy woman pacing beneath a nearby tree. She's been shadowing our footsteps all morning, delivering so many cups of coffee I'm a little worried about my blood pressure. "Everything okay?"

"Ginny called me a little while ago." Violet nods

toward her coworker. "She said something about plans to remove the brush behind the clinic? It had her worried."

Tristan frowns as he crosses his arms over his chest. "Why? There's nothing to worry about. It's a good thing. Deacon's going to remove the brush and build dry creek beds there, instead. Come fire season, the lack of tinder will help protect the building and animals in case a wildfire gets too close." He jabs a thumb over his shoulder. "I'm going to get sprinklers installed on the roof, too."

"That's wonderful." Violet's brow wrinkles. "But we discovered a colony of California tiger salamanders living behind the paddocks last year. They're endangered in Sonoma County and pretty rare in California in general. Taking out the brush and digging trenches would destroy their habitat, wipe out the entire population."

Tristan sighs, dragging a hand through his hair. "Crap. Why didn't she say anything? I had no idea."

"She didn't think you would listen," Violet whispers, her gaze darting my way as she adds, "and I think she was a little intimidated by Deacon."

"No need to be," I say, shooting a smile Virginia's way, which is met with obvious suspicion. I turn back to Tristan. "Sounds like we need to put a pin in this for a while. See if there are any laws on the books protecting the habitat. You don't want to get hit with a fine. Some of them are pretty severe."

"You don't want to kill innocent, endangered salamanders, either," Violet pipes up, glaring up at me with narrow-eyed disapproval that's becoming all too familiar.

"Agreed," I say with a nod. "This plan was about protecting animals and property, not putting a native population in danger. We'll have to come up with a Plan B."

The surprise that sweeps across Violet's face, softening every tight muscle, would be funny if it weren't further confirmation that she thinks the worst of me.

"Got it," Tristan says. "Let me put in a quick call to my guy at fish and wildlife. Do you have a second to hang out, Deacon? See if I can get any info from Don?"

"I've got lots of seconds." I reach for the door, holding it open for Tristan and Violet, who, after a beat of hesitation, drifts closer, pausing to look at me, her eyes searching mine. "What's up?" I ask, voice huskier than it was before. Standing this close to her still affects me, no matter how much I wish it didn't.

"I'm just..." She pauses, pulling in a deeper breath. "Thank you. For listening and being so understanding. This is really important to Ginny. And to me."

"Me, too," I say. "Contrary to what some people might think, I'm not a brainless cretin who enjoys killing animals for sport. I've actually got a soft spot for just about all living things." I shrug. "Except hornets."

Violet nods seriously. "Well, yeah. Hornets are awful. I mean, lots of other insects have stingers, but they're not aggressive jerks who go around attacking people all the time. Hornets need to relax."

"They do." I attempt to keep my tone neutral, but apparently, I do a shit job of it.

Or maybe Violet's just a mind reader.

"Point taken," she says, with a sigh. "I apologize for making unkind assumptions. For what it's worth, I'm not usually this prickly. I think we just got off on the wrong foot, rubbed each other the wrong way or something."

I arch a meaningful brow, and Violet's cheeks go pink.

"Well, right." She flicks a lock of hair from her forehead as her gaze shifts sharply to the left. "Obviously not all the time. Sometimes we rub each other okay."

I know I shouldn't say a word—I'm done with this woman, remember?—but I can't help asking, "Just okay?"

Her flush deepens, spreading pink to the tip of her nose as she mutters, "Point taken again. I should probably get inside, see if Tristan needs any help."

"After you." I nod toward the door I'm still holding, and Violet scurries past, crossing the empty waiting room and disappearing through the door leading to the office area and the animal quarters beyond.

I cross to a couch by the wall and take a seat, grabbing a copy of Sonoma County Weekly and staring at it in a vain attempt to stop thinking about all the ways I would like to keep rubbing Violet the right way. But it's no use. The words smear and swirl, my brain too busy replaying every kiss Violet and I have shared the past few days to leave any bandwidth for reading.

I'm still on the first page of an article about goat cheese ice cream when Virginia slips through the door, gliding across the blue and white tiles to disappear into the office as well.

Not two seconds later, I hear her whisper, "What's

happening? Do we need to call the cops? Stage a sit-in? Get Greenpeace involved?"

"No, they're going to make another plan," Violet says, her voice carrying unexpectedly well, too. It's quiet in here, but I wouldn't have thought I'd be able to hear them from this far away. I consider moving to a chair closer to the door or heading outside to wait for Tristan, but instead, I stay put, too curious about what Violet's going to say about me behind my back to resist the urge to eavesdrop.

"Both Tristan and Deacon want to make sure the population is protected," she continues. "Everything's going to be fine."

"Really?" Virginia huffs in disbelief. "Well…who would have thought? I figured a firefighter would only care about stopping the fire, forget the animals who might be hurt in the process. Especially salamanders. People don't usually care about amphibians the way they care about cute fluffy things with fur."

"Well, sometimes people surprise you," Violet says, a wistfulness in her voice that makes me wonder if maybe…

Just maybe…

Ginny harrumphs. "Yeah, too bad it's usually in the bad way. You still talking to that dating-app guy who stood you up?"

"No. I deleted our chat history and put my profile on a break. I'm considering deleting the app altogether. Yes, it's hard to meet people in real life, but I seriously doubt I'm going to find what I'm looking for online."

"Absolutely not," Ginny agrees without missing a beat. "If that guy looked as good as his pictures, he would have shown up for the in-person meeting. He's probably a troll who's been living under a bridge for twenty years and has forgotten how to shower or clip his toenails."

"Gross." Violet laughs. "But I'm not really worried about that. I mean, yes, I'd like someone who's pleasant to look at, but I'd also like someone who's kind and thoughtful. Someone who makes me laugh and think and who's fun to spend time with, you know? The whole package. And I'd like to be his whole package, too."

Virginia grumbles something I can't make out beneath her breath, and Violet laughs again. "You're probably right, but I don't want to compromise. I'd rather be alone than be with someone who doesn't check my boxes. Especially kindness. That's non-negotiable."

"And showering," Ginny adds.

Violet hums thoughtfully. "Yes, and showering. Which reminds me, I think there's a leak under the dog wash station. I keep finding mysterious puddles every time I..."

Her voice fades away as she and Ginny apparently move away from the front desk, making further eavesdropping impossible. But I've already heard the good stuff, the stuff that has me on my feet, still pacing the waiting room when Tristan emerges from his office ten minutes later.

"Sorry to keep you waiting," he says. "Don put me on hold to see if he could get his hands on guidelines for moving forward, but there are only a few colonies of these salamanders left in California. They're so rare that none of his people are sure what to do next. He's going to put out some feelers and get back to me with options for dealing with the brush while still maintaining habitat. But we're on hold for now."

"No worries," I say, too distracted by nagging questions to focus on fire prevention. "Would you say I'm kind? In general?"

Tristan smiles, cocking his head as he says, "Of course. I mean, you're grouchy sometimes, but never in a mean way. Why?"

"And fun to spend time with?" I ask, ignoring his question. "I know I'm not a laugh riot, but I can show someone a good time when I put my mind to it."

"Sure," Tristan says, studying me with increasing suspicion. "Is there a reason you're fishing for compliments this morning? Or you just need a self-esteem boost after spending so much time with Dad the past few weeks?"

I shrug. "Nope. No reason."

His eyes narrow. "Liar."

"I'm not a liar. I'm keeping confidential intel confidential."

"Good luck with that. You're not in the service anymore, big brother," Tristan says, backing toward the office. "People talk around here, and gossip spreads faster than wildfire."

I *humph* in response, but I know he's right. The second I make a serious play for Violet, everyone we know will know about it. There are no secrets in this town or this family. If I'm going to give this a shot, might as well be upfront about it from the beginning.

"What would you think about me asking one of your

employees on a date?" I ask softly, just in case Violet or Virginia have wandered back into earshot.

"I'd say that Ginny's a little old for you, but that love can work miracles," Tristan says, a shit-eating grin on his face.

"You know that's not who I'm talking about."

"I know." His grin stretches wider. "Violet's number is on one of the fliers on the corkboard. She teaches pottery classes in her spare time. I'm sure she wouldn't mind getting a text from the most eligible bachelor in Sonoma County."

I roll my eyes. Hard.

"It's true, big bro," Tristan insists, aiming a finger in my direction and pulling the trigger. "Now that I'm off the market, anyway. Touch base with you when I hear from Don. Let me know if you need help flirting via text." He pauses, frowning as he adds, "Or calling. Were phones even invented the last time you were dating?"

I flip him the bird, he laughs, and I head for the door.

I don't intend to stop by the corkboard—if Violet wanted me to have her number, I'd have it already—but my hand reaches out of its own free will, ripping one of the remaining rectangles from the bottom of the page. My hand doesn't care about looking overeager or getting shot down a fourth time by the same woman. My hand just wants to touch her again.

I tug my cell out of my back pocket on the way to my truck, figuring there's no point in waiting. Now is as good a time to be shot down as any. Punching in Violet's digits, I shoot off a quick message—*You're right.*

We got off on the wrong foot. But maybe it's not too late to get on the right one. Can I take you to lunch today?

I don't expect an answer anytime soon—she's at work, and I'm sure she'll need some time to decide how best to let me down easy. But before I can slide my phone back into my pocket, it makes a swooping sound.

I look down to see—*Lunch sounds nice. Want to meet somewhere in town around twelve thirty?*

A grin tugging at my lips, I text back—*I'll pick you up. That way we'll only have to worry about parking one car. Looking forward to it.*

She responds with a thumbs-up, a smiley face emoji, and a *Me, too*.

Win. Big win. Not really. Actually, kind of a small win.

Still, it feels pretty damned good.

CHAPTER 10

VIOLET

his isn't a date. It isn't even close to a date.

It's just lunch, the midday repast and least interesting of all meals.

Dinner begs to be lingered over. Breakfast is the start of a bright and beautiful new day. Lunch is something you throw in your mouth to keep your blood sugar stable while you're busy getting shit done.

And I have tons of shit to get done, a fact I'm reminded of as Deacon pulls into a spot on the street near the weekly farmer's market, currently in full swing in the adjacent parking lot.

"I should pick up lettuce and carrots before we head back." I jump out of the truck, even though I'm pretty sure Deacon is an "open a lady's door" kind of guy. But having my door opened would confirm that this was more than a friendly lunch, and I'm not ready for that.

I'm still not sure why I said "yes" to meeting up in the first place. Temporary insanity? A momentary lapse in judgment? Or am I just that much of a soft touch when it comes to people showing kindness to my friends and salamanders?

Soft touch. No doubt about it.

But that doesn't mean I should drop my guard completely. Deacon has given me plenty of reasons to keep my defenses in place. At least for now.

"And radishes if they have any," I continue. "Maybe some asparagus. We're out of bunny treats at the shelter."

"Not a problem," Deacon says, circling around the front of the truck.

He stops just a hair too close, and I cross my arms over my chest, putting an extra barrier between my nipples and his raw animal magnetism.

Oh God, why am I here? Why did I agree to have lunch with this man who turns me into a feral sex monster every time he gets near enough for his delicious scent to invade my space bubble? What if I start humping his leg under the table at the sandwich shop or something equally embarrassing? It sounds ridiculous, but I'm not my usual relatively level-headed self when I'm around Deacon Hunter.

"I mean, if you're not in a rush," I add as he shifts even closer, making my pulse race as he pushes the truck door closed behind me, summoning a nervous laugh from my lips. "Sorry. I thought I'd closed it."

"No worries." He smiles down at me, making it even harder to breathe. "I'm not in a rush. Now that we have salamanders to consider, I've got the entire day free."

My tongue slips out to dampen my lips. "Salamanders to Consider. That would be a great band name."

He smiles, and I see stars, fireworks exploding in the

blue sky behind his even deeper blue eyes. Damn, he's pretty when he smiles.

"It would," he agrees. "But what kind of music would STC play?"

"Country maybe? Bluegrass?"

"Bluegrass with an old-school indie rock edge. Ben Folds Five meets Allison Kraus and Union Station."

I nod slowly, a grin curving my lips. "That would actually be pretty amazing. The more I think about it, the more I like it. So you're pretty into music?"

"I am. I play with a band when I'm in town. Mostly classic rock, but we add some country into the mix every once in a while."

"That's amazing," I say, delighted and ashamed of myself at the same time. I've definitely jumped to some unfair conclusions where Deacon is concerned. "I'd like to come and hear you play sometime. Classic rock is my favorite dancing music."

"I know this about you," he says, making me blush for the third or fourth time today and reminding me that he's still the man who tried to boss me off a dance floor. The fact that he ended up being right about the potential danger at the Raven Claw doesn't excuse the fact that he barged in and started giving orders like I was a child in his care instead of another adult capable of calmly discussing his concerns.

"Maybe we could go dancing some time," he says, throwing me for a loop all over again.

"You dance?" I arch a brow.

He inclines his head. "I do. Nothing to write home about, like you, but I move well with others."

I bet you do, I think, even as another part of my brain

blares out a warning that dancing is definitely a date activity, not something new friends would enjoy together on a free weekend.

But would that be so awful?

Just because Deacon and I have spent half of our time together so far fighting like cats and dogs doesn't mean the trend has to continue. People can change. I believe that. I've seen it, both for the worse and for the better.

"Maybe we should go dancing, then," I say breezily as I lean back against the truck, pretending my pulse isn't already discoing in my throat at the thought of spending the evening swaying in Deacon's arms. "But we should probably see if we can make it through lunch without wanting to kill each other first."

His lips lilt into a sleepy smile that ramps up the flood of hormones rushing through my bloodstream. "I never want to kill you. Just strangle you a little. Gently. Until you stop fighting with me and let me kiss you again."

I try to bite back a grin and fail. "The kissing is nice."

"Nice isn't the word I would use," he says, the look in his eyes making every nerve ending in my body hum as he braces his arms on either side of my face.

"What word would you use?"

"Incredible." He holds my gaze with an intensity that takes my breath away. "Amazing. Sweet." He tips his head closer to mine. "I know I'm not your idea of a dream date, Violet. But we'd have fun together. And maybe I could help you forget about being lonely for a while."

"I'm not lonely," I lie, lifting my chin and fighting, with everything in me, the urge to press my lips to his. I will *not* make out with him in public in broad daylight. I know too many people in this town, and I'm not sure what will happen the next time his lips meet mine.

"Well, I am," Deacon says, the unexpected vulnerability making my heart go soft and achy around the edges. "My boys are off at college, and the rest of my friends and family have lives they built while I was deployed on and off for twenty years. I spend a lot of my time feeling like I'm on the outside looking in. I could use some company. A friend. Or, maybe more than a friend…"

My hands drift to his chest, molding to his powerful muscles without my conscious permission. But he just feels so good, so oddly familiar, even though we've really only known each other—more than to say hello to —for less than a week. Still, chemistry isn't a guarantee that we'd work as friends, let alone anything more. "What if we can't find anything to talk about?"

"I don't think that'll be a problem. But if it is, then we don't have to talk," he whispers. And then he kisses me. His lips capture mine for a slow, deep, oh-so-sexy kiss that turns my bones to jelly and ratchets up the aching between my legs to an intensity that's almost painful.

But sweet, too…

Painfully sweet.

I kiss him back with everything in me, fisting my fingers in his soft shirt and pulling him closer, even though my gut insists I'm going to regret this. Regret it like that third piece of birthday cake, the one that leaves you sick to your stomach and cursing yourself for taking too much of a good thing.

Deacon is too much of a good thing, and definitely way more than a woman who hasn't dated since she was a teenager is prepared to handle.

But when he pulls away, leaving me trembling with wanting him after just one kiss, I nod my spinning head. "All right. Let's do dinner. Tonight. My place. Six o'clock. But you have to be gone by eight when my daughter gets home."

"Or we could go out," he says. "I'd like to buy you a meal."

"I don't want you to buy me a meal, I want you to kiss me until all of my clothes come off," I confess in a rush. "I haven't been able to sleep for days. I can barely eat. All I can think about is touching you, kissing you. Doing more than kiss you…"

"Me, too," he confesses, a haunted look on his face that I completely understand. "I was starting to think I'd have to sign up for an Iron Man Triathlon to get you out of my head."

I grin. "Yeah?"

"Yeah," he says, his lips curving. "You look pretty pleased with yourself, Ms. Boden. Do you enjoy torturing men with your insane sex vibe?"

I grin harder. "Well, you know what they say, misery loves company."

"So does pleasure." He winks. "I'll be at your place at six sharp."

"Good," I say, a shiver of excitement whispering across my skin. "I'll text you the address after lunch."

"Yeah. Lunch. Let's get to that. I'm starving. What

are you in the mood for? Barbeque? A sandwich from Oakville Grocery?"

I arch a brow. "What if I said I wanted a tofu scramble from Vegan Voodoo? With a kale and kiwi smoothie?"

"I'd say that sounds disgusting," he says without missing a beat, "but I'd give it a try. I'll try anything once. Twice if there's a beautiful woman involved." He steps back, holding out a hand as he nods toward the town square. "You ready?"

Am I ready? Hell, no.

I'm not sure I'm ready for casual dating, let alone whatever this is Deacon and I are about to jump into. Enemies with benefits? Friends who rip each other's clothes off every chance they get? Addicts mutually hooked on each other's kiss?

I have no idea, but it's too late to turn back now. I couldn't resist this man if I tried, and I don't want to even attempt to say no.

I reach out, taking his hand, twining my fingers through his much larger ones with a nod. "Ready."

Or not. But here we go…

CHAPTER 11

From the texts of Deacon Hunter
and Tristan Hunter

Tristan: Just heard from Don. He's going to need the rest of the week to sort this out, find a specialist, etc. So we're in a holding pattern for now. Sorry again. I hate that you drove all the way out to Healdsburg for nothing.

Deacon: It's fine. We're past peak fire season. We don't have to rush, and I've got nothing but time.

Tristan: What about the fire department? I thought you were getting ready to go two days on, three days off?

Deacon: I won't know if I got the promotion for another week or two. Until then, I'm still part-time, working a couple afternoons here and there when they need management help.

Tristan: Sounds like a sweet gig to me. If I had your pension, I'd be fishing every morning. Let the rest of us suckers do the nine-to-five gig.

Deacon: Yeah, that was fun for the first few weeks. Now I'm bored out of my skull. With the boys gone and Dad and Dylan handling most everything at the farm, I'm ready to jump into something new.

Tristan: Speaking of something new… I wasn't going to ask, but Zoey is dying to know how your date went with Violet.

Deacon: It wasn't a date. It was lunch. But I'd say it went well. We're going to have dinner together tonight.

Tristan: TWO MEALS IN A ROW! OMG, that's so exciting!!! This is Zoey, by the way! I stole Tristan's phone because I knew he wouldn't use enough exclamation points to express how wonderful this is!! Isn't Violet amazing?!

Deacon: She is. Very beautiful and very smart.

Tristan: And the sweetest person you'll ever meet! And gorgeous and talented and funny and I just know you two are going to have so much fun together!!

Deacon: I hope so. Not sure we have much in common, but I'm looking forward to getting to know her better.

Tristan: What?! You two have loads in common! You

both have grown kids, you're both ridiculously good looking, you both think Tristan and I are too nice most of the time, you both have well-developed artistic sides, and you both love hard apple cider. That's five things, right off the top of my head.

Deacon: I stand corrected.

Tristan: Good, because I like the two of you together. I know you'll be nice to her, not like the other jerks she's been dating since she and her ex-husband called it quits. Single men over forty sound like the absolute pits, Deacon. No offense.

Deacon: None taken. Though, I'll add that single women over forty can be a handful, too. We're all a little too set in our ways at this point to be very good company.

Tristan: Not true. You're great company, and Violet is one of my favorite souls on earth. Some people get better with age. You'll see. This is going to be epic! But no pressure, of course.
So don't be nervous.
Though, you should know that if you break her heart, I will be forced to put Ex-Lax in your birthday cake next year. Sisters before misters, even if the mister is a brother-in-law.

Deacon: Of course. Understood.

Tristan: You want me to hand the phone back to Tristan?

Deacon: No thanks, Zoey, I'm good.

Tristan: Are you sure? Tristan is happy to help.

Deacon: Really, I'm good. All good.

CHAPTER 12

DEACON

I'm not good. I'm not anything close to good.

Five times, I almost call Violet to cancel.

Yes, I've been fantasizing about having her naked and under me pretty much constantly since that first kiss on Halloween. But after texting with Zoey, it's clear I've underestimated how close she and Violet are, and the last thing I want is to have my sister-in-law pissed at me for the rest of our lives because I did her best friend wrong.

Not that I plan on doing Violet wrong. Quite the contrary—I intend to do her oh-so-fucking-right—but relationships don't always pan out as planned, especially relationships with sex involved.

If I were thinking clearly, I'd call Violet, explain the conflict, and move on.

But I don't want to move on. I want to move in. I want my mouth on every inch of Violet Boden like I want peace in the Middle East.

Fine, *more* than I want peace in the Middle East. I

deployed to Saudi Arabia enough times to know a lasting resolution to all the conflict brewing over there isn't in the cards anytime soon, but Violet Boden is right around the corner. Just a ten-minute drive from my house and two right turns...

I pull up in front of her place—a two-story blue craftsman with stars painted across the front that's as cute as she is—at ten 'til six with a growler of Pink Lady apple cider. And I swear, it's all I can do not to jump out of the truck and take the steps to her front door two at a time. I'm not in any condition to play it cool with this woman. I want her too much. I'm feverish with it, my thoughts so cloudy it's been hard to think of anything but her scent, her skin, her fingers tangling in my hair as she pulls me closer to her mouth.

I'd be ashamed of myself if I weren't pretty sure that she's caught it, too, this mysterious lust sickness that's laid me low.

As I turn off the ignition, her front door opens, revealing Violet in a little black dress, with her long hair wild around her shoulders and fire in her eyes. She's clearly been waiting for me, but her feet are bare. So is her mouth, without a trace of lipstick in sight.

I slam out of the truck and start up the walk, watching her toes curl against the hardwood floor and her teeth dig into her bottom lip. Oh yeah, dinner is going to have to wait. Drinks, too.

Tonight, we're skipping straight to dessert.

I jog up the front porch steps, she takes the cider and my keys from me without a word, setting them on a bright green table just inside the door with a relieved sound that echoes the emotion rushing through my chest. A beat later she's in my arms, her lips hot on my mine as I bury my hands in her hair. We stumble into the room, kissing harder, deeper as Violet's fingers get busy with the buttons on my flannel and my hands smooth up her thighs to grip her ass through her panties.

They're as silky as her hair and held together with tiny strings of fabric on the side, and I'm pretty sure I'm going to have a heart attack when she moans into my mouth and rocks her hips forward, pressing against where my cock is straining against the seam of my zipper. I'm in the best shape of my life. I run almost every morning, lift weights, and swim at least three times a week. Hell, a few weeks ago I scaled Mount Whitney with some old climbing friends from the Air Force, beating our last ascent time by several hours, proving we're not letting retirement slow us down.

But none of my training has prepared me for what Violet Boden does to me. For the way she makes my heart pound and my head spin and every cell in my body cry out for satisfaction. Liberation.

"It feels like I'm dying," she pants, head falling back as I kiss my way down her neck and she drags my flannel off my shoulders. "Like I'm going to die if I don't have you inside me."

I growl my agreement as my hand dives further beneath her dress. I glide over the warm skin of her stomach, the delicate ridges of her ribs to cup her breast. "And you just might kill me," I say, rubbing my thumb over her tight nipple, drawing a soft, hungry sound from her lips that makes me even hotter, hungrier. "If you keep running around without a bra on, looking so fucking sexy I want to tear your clothes off with my teeth."

"Oh yes, do that," she says, tugging my undershirt up to my chest. "Your teeth, your hands, whatever, just get them off."

I lift my arms, bending my knees to make it easier for her to pull my shirt up the rest of the way. The moment my hands are free, I attack her dress, ripping it up and over her head, sending her hair flying around her shoulders as I fall to my knees in front of her, kissing and biting her stomach, her hip, as I rub my fingers over her clit through her panties with one hand and cup her bare breast with the other.

"Oh my God," she murmurs as she leans back, bracing her arms on the counter behind her.

I don't remember how we got into the kitchen. I couldn't tell you what the rest of it looks like, I only know that her golden skin glows against the creamy white of the cabinet and I suddenly can't think of a better place to feast on this woman who drives me out of my goddamned mind.

I press my face against her mound through the silk, inhaling the tart, salty scent of her arousal as I draw the crotch of her panties aside and glide two fingers into where she's so hot and wet.

"I love this," I breathe, voice tight with the effort it's taking to restrain myself, at least a little bit. "I love how wet you get for me, Violet, how your body begs for this." I push deeper, curling my fingers to rub against that place inside her that makes her knees go weak. "I can't wait to taste you again."

She calls my name, trembling as she grips handfuls

of my hair. "No. You. Please, I want you inside me. So much. Please. Right now. Right fucking now."

I'm hooking my fingers in the side-strings of her panties, about to rip them down her legs, lift her onto the counter, and give her exactly what she's asking for, when a door slams and a high-pitched voice calls out, "Mom, come quick!"

Violet and I jerk apart so fast it's like someone tossed a lit firecracker between us.

"Georgia hit a dog with her car on the way to get sandwiches," the girl continues, moving deeper into the house as I reach for my shirt and Violet snatches her dress from the floor. "We tried to take him to the vet on College by the car wash, but they were already closed. Are you upstairs?"

"In the kitchen, honey," Violet calls out in a surprisingly steady voice as we both hurry back into our recently-discarded clothes. "And don't worry. Dr. Moshin doesn't close until seven on weeknights. We've still got time."

I barely have time to tug my flannel back on and run a quick hand through my hair when a mini Violet with pink streaks in her ponytail appears around the corner. "Seriously, it's awful, Mom, the poor thing just—" Her words cut off and her eyes—blue instead of Violet's brown—go wide as they land on me. "Oh. I'm sorry. I didn't know anyone else was here."

"This is Deacon," Violet says, nodding my way. "He's with the handyman service. He's here to fix the oven. Deacon, this is my daughter Adriana."

I lift a hand. "Hello, Adriana."

"Hi," she says, her brows drawing together as she

shifts her attention back to Violet. "I didn't know the oven was broken."

Violet shrugs. "Yeah, it wouldn't get hot for some reason."

"Wouldn't get hot," Adriana echoes, clearly still suspicious.

"No, it wouldn't." Violet reaches out, patting my shoulder. "But Deacon fixed it. Now it heats up just fine."

I duck my head, hiding a smile.

"Now, let's go see this dog," she continues, starting out of the kitchen. "It didn't bite either of you, did it?"

"No, Mom. It's a sweet little thing." The eye-roll in her daughter's voice is all-too-familiar. The boys don't hit me with that tone much anymore, but their junior and senior years of high school were a different story.

"Well, even sweet little things can bite when they're hurt or scared, and he could have rabies for all we know." Violet grabs a throw blanket off the top of a pile near the cozy-looking couch where I'd hoped to be devouring her pussy for dessert. Sadly, it seems fate has other plans for us tonight.

I'm about to offer my goodbyes and head for the door when it flies open and a second girl—a curly-haired kid with tears streaming down her honey-brown cheeks—appears, silhouetted against the darkening sky. "My car died! I can't get it to start again, Addie. It's dead, and the dog is almost dead, and this is the worst day of my entire life!"

She dissolves into shuddery sobs, Adriana's eyes fill with tears, and a pained, helpless expression flashes across Violet's face. Instantly, I know I'm not going anywhere. I'm not leaving her alone with two hysterical kids and a dying dog, not even if she begs me to.

"We'll take my truck," I say, grabbing my keys from the table by the door. "We'll get the little guy settled and be there in ten minutes."

"You don't have to, Deacon," Violet begins, "I can take them in my car, I—"

"More room in the truck," I cut her off, holding up the keys. "You want to drive, since you know the way? And I'll hold the patient?"

Relief flickers in her eyes. "Okay. Yes." She reaches for her keys and motions the girls toward the street. "You two get in the truck. Deacon and I will be there in just a minute. The dog is in the back seat of your car, Georgia?"

Georgia nods, swiping a hand across her tear-streaked face. "Yes, but he's not moving, Miss V. I'm scared it's already too late. I'm afraid I killed him. He just ran out into the street so fast, I didn't have time to stop."

Violet puts a hand on her back, rubbing in circles as she guides the girl down the stairs. "It's going to be okay, honey. Accidents happen. It's not your fault."

"The most important thing is that you two are okay," I say, starting toward the VW Bug parked behind Violet's Prius in the driveway. I'm planning what to do if the dog is already dead—wrap him in a towel, let the girls say goodbye, and take him back to the farm for a proper burial—when I open the door to find two melted chocolate eyes peering up at me from the tan seat.

"There you are, buddy," I say softly. "You're going to be all right."

The pup—a corgi with some mutt mixed in—gives a weak wag of its tail and Violet coos softly behind me, "Oh, what a sweetheart. We're going to get you fixed up, pumpkin. Don't worry." She presses the blanket into my hands as she adds in a whisper, "I think one or both of his back legs might be broken."

"I'll be gentle," I promise.

"I know you will," she says, resting a hand on the small of my back. "Thank you."

Before I can assure her that there's no need for thanks, she's gone, hurrying back to my truck where the girls are already climbing into the back cab. I watch her for a beat—my heart aching for some inexplicable reason—and then turn back to the dog.

Best to stay focused on the emergency at hand. There will be time later to worry that I might be developing something more serious than a sex addiction to Violet Boden.

CHAPTER 13

VIOLET

*B*y the time we get Dash to the vet—Adriana insists on naming him, assuring Georgia that the magic of a new name will keep the little guy from crossing over the rainbow bridge—get him checked out, and fill out the paperwork for Dr. Moshin to board him while he's under observation for a broken leg and internal injuries, it's eight thirty and the girls are both weak from hunger. Adriana's stomach is growling so loud I can hear it over the hum of the traffic on College Avenue.

"Everyone okay with tacos?" Deacon asks, guiding the truck into the parking lot of Viva Taqueria.

The man is so bossy he can even turn questions into orders.

A tiny voice in my head reminds me that I loathe that about him, but I'm not feeling anything close to loathing for the man who orders the family pack meal and limeade for four and gets up twice for extra napkins when the girls prove incapable of keeping their salsa inside their carne asada tacos.

No, not loathing. Not irritation.

The emotion spreading through my chest like honey is warm, soft, and as sweet as the jasmine-scented air outside my house. It teases at my nose as I stand in the drive, watching Deacon jumpstart Georgia's ancient bug and give her strict instructions not to turn off the car until she gets home.

"And tell your parents you probably just need a new battery," he says. "I'd try that before taking it into the shop."

"Thanks." Georgia beams up at him from the driver's seat. "It's just my mom and me. But my mom is great with cars. She rebuilt the engine for this one herself."

"Sounds like you're in good hands, then," Deacon says.

Georgia nods. "And she's a really good cook. And an amazing dancer. You should get her number from Miss V, maybe. If you're single."

I lift a hand to my face, concealing a smile as Deacon's eyes go wide.

"Don't see no wedding ring," Adriana says, darting past Deacon to kiss Georgia's cheek. "I'll get him hooked up with Mama Jay's digits, just in case. You drive safe. And don't forget about the Calc quiz."

Georgia groans as she shifts into reverse. "Ugh. This day. Can it just be over already?"

"Almost there!" Adriana encourages, pumping her fist in the air as Georgia pulls out. She waits until the VW Bug glides away before turning back to pin Deacon with a hard look. "You don't want Miss Jay's number, do you?"

Deacon shakes his head. "No, thank you."

"Good." Adriana crosses her arms at her chest. "Because that would be weird. Considering you're dating my mom and all."

My lips part on a denial, but Adriana is already waving a hand in my direction.

"Save it, Mom. I'm not stupid, and you're the worst liar ever. The stove wouldn't heat up…" She rolls her eyes. "Seriously, a two-year-old could have seen through that one. Not to mention the googly eyes."

I huff. "I do not have googly eyes."

"No, but he does." Adriana jabs a thumb toward Deacon with a grin. "You think my mom is soooo pretty."

"Beautiful, not pretty," Deacon says, not missing a beat.

My cheeks go hot, and I instantly know I'm in trouble.

"Aw, look! And now Mom's blushing," Adriana says, going in for the kill, as expected. "You guys are gross and cute and I approve. Now, I have to go study. Thanks for the help and the dinner, Deacon. You seem super cool, but if you hurt my mom, I'll hurt your face."

"Understood." Deacon lifts a hand. "Good to meet you, Adriana."

"You, too," she chirps as she turns to me with a wink. "If you have plans tonight, Mom, I'm fine to stay by myself. I can set an alarm and get up on time when I put my mind to it."

I shake my head. "I'll be right in. We're watching a

movie, remember?" She starts to argue, but I cut her off, "No, you're not staying by yourself. Go inside. And just remember, the more you embarrass me now, the more I embarrass you when you bring your next boyfriend over."

Addie pales, looking so upset by the joke I'm about to apologize and assure her I'm only kidding when her grin pops back into place. "Good thing I have no plans to bring a boy over any time soon. And that I'm not easily embarrassed. Later, Deacon. See you inside, Mom." She turns, trotting up the porch, her words leaving me feeling strangely deflated.

She used to blush bright red at the drop of a hat. Of all my girls, Adriana was always the most sensitive, but sometime in the past year, that's changed. She's changed so much that sometimes I feel like I'm running to catch up with this confident new person she's becoming. This person with a secret boyfriend she apparently has no intention of introducing me to in the near future.

"You okay?" Deacon shifts closer, stepping into the glow from the streetlamp.

I nod, forcing a smile. "Yeah. It's just hard. She used to tell me everything and need her Mama so much, and now..." I glance back at the house, dropping my voice. "Now she's in a relationship she doesn't talk about, and keeps secrets from me constantly, and I wonder if we'll ever be close like that again."

"You will be. She loves you, and girls always need their mothers." He sighs. "It's boys you have to worry about. They'll head off into the world, fall in love, and forget all about the old man who raised them."

I lean into him, nudging his arm with my shoulder. "You're not an old man."

"I feel like one sometimes. Like when the twins are lecturing me on how to work that stupid SnapTalk app they like to use instead of calling. Or Caleb has to install the new operating system on my computer after I've crashed the damn thing five times."

I smile. "Okay, so maybe you are an old man. But you're a sexy old man, so at least you've got that going for you."

Deacon laughs, a low rumble that makes my skin hum as he draws me into his arms. "Good. Glad I'm not a complete lost cause."

"Not even a little bit." I wrap my arms around his neck. "You're growing on me, Mr. Hunter. Thanks for being so wonderful tonight."

"Just being a decent human being."

"You were much more than decent," I insist. "You were generous and patient and calm in the face of teenage girl tears. You deserve a medal for courage under fire during a shit show of a first date."

"Does that mean I get a second one?" he asks, his eyes flashing. "I'd really like to see more of you."

"I'd like to see more of you, too," I breathe, my heart fluttering in my throat as memories of how close we got to banging in my kitchen flicker on my mental screen. "Is tomorrow night too soon?"

"Tomorrow night is perfect," he says. "I'll pick you up at six? We'll grab dinner?"

I lift a shoulder and arch a brow. "Or I could come to your place for dinner. Addie will be home tomorrow night so we wouldn't have privacy here, but I hear your kids are already at college, so…"

He shakes his head. "No, ma'am. I need to take you out. That's the only way I'm keeping my hands off of you long enough to eat."

"Well, eating is kind of overrated, isn't it?"

"Not all eating," he says with a bob of his brows that makes his meaning clear.

"Gross." I huff and roll my eyes, but I'm smiling when I say, "I'm a lady on the street, Mr. Hunter. Save your dirty jokes for my kitchen, where they belong."

His laugh is a deep, easy rumble that warms me all over, so cozy that it doesn't seem strange when he bends down, pressing an oh-so-tender kiss to my forehead.

It's an affectionate kiss, not a hungry kiss. Unprecedented for us, but…I like it.

I like it so much that when he says, "Let me take you out. I want to buy you a meal, look at your pretty face across the table, and torture myself a little dreaming about what I'm going to do to you when I get you back to my place," I nod.

"Okay." I hold his gaze, my pulse pumping faster. "But pick me up in the diner parking lot at the end of the block, okay? I'll meet you there. I don't want Addie getting any ideas."

"Ideas about you dating again? Because I think that ship has already sailed."

"No, ideas about me being gone for a significant amount of time. I'll tell her I'm going for coffee with my friend Mina or something, that way she won't know when I'm getting back and will hopefully stay put in her room studying instead of sneaking out to meet whoever she's been meeting."

Deacon frowns. "If you need to stay home with her, I understand. We can meet up another time."

"No, she's eighteen. She's fine to be home alone," I say, before adding in a softer voice, "besides, I want to see you again."

"I want to see you again, too." He draws me closer, kissing me one last time. But it doesn't feel like a goodbye kiss. It feels like hello and the start of something new.

CHAPTER 14

DEACON

*S*he's all I can think about.

All day long, as I help Dad fix a hole in the fence at the back of the property and make a run to town for groceries and gasoline for the tractor, my thoughts are a million miles away.

Or twenty-two miles away, to be precise, at the Better Way shelter, where Violet is busy supervising cat socialization. She sends me pictures of the skittish-looking and downright irate cats, along with captions that have me laughing aloud more than once. They also give me an excuse to keep scrolling back through our texts to the picture she sent me this morning, the selfie of her pointing, eyes comically wide, to the kitchen counter where I came so close to being inside her.

I'm pretty sure my kitchen is haunted by the ghost of almost-nookie past, she'd typed beneath. *Excited to see you tonight.*

Excited doesn't begin to cover it.

I'm out of my head. Out of my mind. Drunk with

anticipation and dizzy with wanting her. I'm an addict in desperate need of a fix.

But I want more than a one-night stand. There's no way I'm getting enough of Violet in one night. That's why we're going to go out and enjoy each other's company before I take her home and devote myself to making her come. I'm going to prove to her that we can have fun together with our clothes on—even if it kills us.

And it just might. I've never heard of anyone dying of lust, but it feels possible.

The hours crawl by at sloth speed until fire ants are crawling beneath my skin. I'm sporting a semi most of the afternoon, and by the time I jump in the shower at four, I'm in a dire state. I almost jerk off under the hot spray—just to take the edge off before I'm exposed to Violet's explosive sex vibe again—but in the end, some sick part of me insists on suffering.

I don't want to come in my own hand to fantasies of Violet. I want to come buried inside her, with her legs wrapped around my waist and her kiss on my lips and those sexy sounds she makes lighting me up the way no music ever has.

And I love music. Music is the one thing in my life that has never let me down.

I've had my share of shit days on the job and dud sessions at the gym, and I won't even get started on failed relationships—familial and romantic. But the moment I pick up my guitar, I'm there in my happy place, where there's nothing but the strings beneath my fingers and the melody in the air. My guitar has saved my life a few times, right after my divorce and later, when I was deployed and missing the twins so much it felt like someone had carved out some vital organ. Playing my favorite songs always brought me back from the edge.

But there's something about Violet's sigh in my ear, her hum of pleasure against my skin. It reaches down deep inside of me, to a place not even music has ever touched.

It should scare me, I guess. For the sake of my sanity, I should probably avoid this woman like a court marshal. Instead, I dress in my best black button-down and a pair of dark wash jeans and push the speed limit all the way to Santa Rosa.

I get to the diner parking lot fifteen minutes early, but she's already there, standing outside the front door, cupping a coffee in her hands, looking good enough to eat in a fuzzy short-sleeved pink sweater, jeans, and cowgirl boots. Beating back a sudden fantasy of Violet in those boots and nothing else, I step down from the truck and cross the lot to meet her.

She spots me coming, and a smile breaks out across her face, a firework lighting up the night sky, so bright and beautiful it makes my heart skip a beat. She's clearly happy to see me, and I haven't been this thrilled to wrap a woman up in my arms in way too damned long.

"You're early," she says, drawing me in for a welcome hug with one arm, all the places where she's seductively soft pressing against me, making me question my sanity all over again.

Why the hell did I insist on dinner again? I'm starting to think I have a masochistic streak I haven't fully explored until now.

"I hope that's all right." I leave my arm around her waist, fingers teasing at the place where the small of her back becomes the curve of her ass. I'm quickly falling in love with this place. I want to kiss it and bite it and mold my fingers over the sweet curve while she's riding me, urging her on with my hand.

"It's perfect," she says. "You can help me finish my hot chocolate."

"Having dessert before dinner?" I lift a brow as I accept the warm mug.

"Yeah, I'm wild like that," she says, her eyes dancing. "Sometimes I'll have nothing but dessert for dinner. Just a bowl of oatmeal cookie dough with extra almonds and raisins mixed in, and a big glass of milk."

I hum around my sip of salty-sweet cocoa. "Raw egg in there, too?"

"Sometimes." She flips her hair over her shoulder. "If I really want to live on the edge."

"Scandalous." I take another drink, shaking my head in mock judgment. "And you look like such a nice girl, too."

"I'm a woman, Mr. Hunter, not a girl."

I sigh, gaze sweeping up and down her curves as she reclaims her cocoa and tips it back, draining the last inch of sweetness. "Yes, you are. I've been thinking about that all day, Ms. Boden."

Her lips quirk as she swallows. "Yeah? About what a grown-up I am?"

"Something like that," I agree.

"I've been thinking about what a grown-up you are, too." Her tongue sweeps across her bottom lip with a shameless sensuality that makes me thicker for the seventy-millionth time today. "So are you sure you wouldn't rather get grilled cheese and French fries to go and head straight back to your place?"

"Grilled cheese and French fries are not good to go foods. They'd be cold and soggy long before we got to Mercyville."

"Something else, then?" She jabs a thumb over her shoulder. "They have all kinds of options. It's not just diner food. They have salads and pasta and a few Greek dishes. I'm sure we can find something up to your standards."

I shake my head. "Nope. I made a reservation. Some-place I think you'll really like."

She cocks her head. "Yeah? That's sweet." Her nose wrinkles as she adds with a smile, "And intriguing. I can't wait to see what you think I like."

"I'm good at reading people," I say. "Almost as good as I am at pissing them off."

She laughs. "Oh good. Then this place should be right up my alley. Just let me return my mug, and we'll get going."

"Perfect," I say, hoping it will be.

When I found the event online earlier today, I didn't hesitate to pick up the phone and secure two tickets. But now, as we drive across the highway to the fair-grounds, I start to second guess myself, an occurrence almost as uncommon as the relentless lust that's been plaguing me since the night I kissed this woman for the first time.

This date feels like a test, and I really don't want to fail.

By the time I park the truck in the lot beside the fairgrounds, my hands are sweating on the wheel. And when Violet leans forward, reading the banner above the entry gates aloud in an even tone, "Welcome to Vegfest, Rock out with your Kale out," I mentally cross my fingers.

I was positive a vegan with such a deep love for animals she's got room in her heart for a colony of salamanders would be way into a food festival, but when I glance her way I can't get a read on her expression. Her eyes are glued to the banner, her lips are pressed tight together, and for the first time since we got into the truck, she's absolutely silent.

I'm about to tell her we can go somewhere else, if she's not into wandering around while she eats, when she turns to me with shining eyes and says, "For almost twenty years, my ex made fun of me for refusing to eat animals, like it was some childish thing I'd gotten into my head and someday I would wake up, grow up and realize it was ridiculous."

My forehead wrinkles. "I'm sorry. That was shitty of him."

"It was. And I never tried to shame him into making the same choices I'd made, I just wanted him to respect them."

I nod. "Absolutely."

"So, this means a lot," she says, motioning toward the entrance. "Thank you."

"I'm not your ex, Violet." I reach out, cupping her face in my hand. "And I happen to really like kale."

She grins. "Me, too. I'm crazy about it. Have it for lunch at least three times a week."

"Sometimes more," I agree, leaning closer. "I like to sauté it with garlic and olive oil and serve it over rice."

"Now you're speaking my language," she purrs.

"Or I'll make a massaged raw kale salad, just rub sesame oil into the leaves with my hands and garnish with—"

"Stop," she says, breath rushing out across my lips. "You're going to get me all worked up, and I'll embarrass myself in front of the veggies."

"Raw kale talk turns you on," I murmur, sliding my fingers into her hair. "Noted. I'll keep that in my back pocket for later, in case I need some help getting you in the mood."

"Never going to happen," she says, hand molding to my chest. "I'm always in the mood when I'm with you."

Before I can tell her the feeling is entirely mutual, she kisses me. And then her tongue sweeps through my mouth, and her fingers dig into my back as she pulls me as close as we can get with the console between us, and I know it's going to be a long night. But a good one.

Something has shifted between us, something subtle but powerful that makes it feel natural to take her hand as we head toward the gates. Natural to rest my hand on her thigh as we perch at bar tables throughout the festival, devouring seaweed salads and mushroom burgers and four different kinds of kale. We even try a kale-infused vodka mixed with cucumber lemon soda that Violet declares, "Weirdly delicious, just like you."

"Weirdly delicious." I cross my arms at my chest, pretending to be offended.

"Unexpectedly delicious?" She slides her arms around me and lifts her face to mine.

"That's better." I kiss her, doing my best to keep it PG, but within a few seconds her tongue is slipping past my lips and my fingers are digging into her ass.

Finally, I drag my mouth away from hers. "Ready to go?"

"Yes, please," she says. "I just need to do one thing first. Be right back."

She dashes away across the sea of tables, toward the booths near the soundstage and the bathrooms beyond. I finish my drink, but the cocktail does nothing to cool the heat gathering inside me. If anything, it makes things worse.

Maybe kale is an aphrodisiac. If so, Violet and I are both in trouble. The last thing we need is any more fuel on this fire.

I'm pulling my phone from my pocket, preparing to investigate the possible erotic properties of kale, when Violet appears at my side and chirps, "For you. A thank you present for a wonderful second date."

She unfurls a rolled up T-shirt, revealing a cartoon leaf with a big grin above the words, "Oh Kale Yeah!" on the front.

I laugh so hard I can barely breathe. I don't know why it cracks me up so much, but it does, and the fact that Violet's giggling along with me, obviously thrilled that her gag gift is a success, only makes things worse. By the time I regain control, my jaw hurts from smiling so hard, I've got a knot in my side, and my chest is full of bubbles.

Happy bubbles that fizz and pop as Violet and I head for the exit arm-in-arm, making my blood feel shot through with sunlight even though the sun went down an hour ago.

CHAPTER 15

VIOLET

I can't remember the last time I laughed this hard, the last time holding hands with someone made me as giddy as a kid on her first date, the last time meeting a man's eye was enough to make me shiver with excitement.

Deacon is something special and so much more fun than I ever expected. He's not just a grouchy alpha male with a highly developed bossy side. He's also sweet and thoughtful and funny and so sexy I'm not sure I'm going to be able to keep my clothes on until we get up to his bedroom.

"My dad's spending the night at his girlfriend's house," he says, nodding toward the empty gravel beside his truck as he shuts off the ignition. "Which means you're spared a game of Twenty Questions. At least for tonight."

"I've met your dad several times." I grab my purse, spilling out of the truck into the cool night air as I add, "I like him. And he likes me."

"But you weren't dating his son before," Deacon says, circling around the back of the truck and holding out a hand I take without hesitation. "He's protective."

"And you're clearly in need of protection," I say, with a pointed look up and down his powerful body. "I mean, how will you ever defend yourself?"

He pauses, grinning as he catches my gaze. "Oh, I don't plan on defending myself. You do whatever you want to me, baby, I'm not going to put up a fight."

I bite my lip. "No? Not even a little one? Just to make things more exciting?"

"I'm going to show you exciting, woman," he says, swooping me into his arms, making me giggle as he jogs up the porch stairs and slams into the house. I barely have time to catch a glimpse of the long wooden table in the dining room and the slightly overwhelming display of antlers above the fireplace mantle before he's climbing the stairs to the second floor.

And then we're in his bedroom and I'm back on my feet, and we're tearing each other's clothes off between kisses as we stumble toward his bed. And then he's on top of me, and his mouth is everywhere, and his hands are everywhere, and I'm drowning in him all over again.

Drowning and burning up with fever at the same time.

I've never wanted anyone the way I want him.

"Now," I beg, crying out as he bites down on my nipple, sending another electric shock of need rippling across my skin. "Please Deacon, inside me now."

He groans in approval of this suggestion, kissing me hard as he positions his gorgeous cock at my entrance and pushes inside. He just...dives in, hard and deep, which would be amazing, except for the fact that it hurts like nobody's business.

"Ow," I squeak, going stiff beneath him as a sharp sting zaps between my legs.

And he stops. Just like that.

Like I've flicked a switch. Not a second of hesitation. He goes still at the end of his next thrust, buried inside of me, but not moving a muscle.

And though the pain is still intense, I find myself flooded with a safe, happy, grateful feeling that makes my heart swell in my chest. And maybe it's a sad statement on my sex life up to this point, but I know for a fact that a lot of men wouldn't have stopped. Men who would have insisted they couldn't stop—the needs of their great and powerful penis were just too overwhelming—or have pretended they didn't hear me.

But not Deacon, this man for whom my pleasure so obviously comes first.

"What's wrong?" He brushes my hair from my face, worried eyes searching mine. "Did I hurt you?"

I shake my head. "No. Well, yes, but it's not your fault. I just...I haven't... It's been a long time, and I guess..." A tight laugh escapes my chest. "I thought my friend Mina was kidding about the whole Divorce Virginity thing, but I guess she wasn't. It really does hurt."

"I'm sorry." He starts to pull out, but I grab the thick muscles of his beautiful backside and hold on tight.

"No, don't leave. I just need a second. I think I would even if you weren't so big."

"Even if I weren't so big?" He smiles down at me as

his fingers trace the curve of my ear to tease the sensitive skin just behind. "Trying to flatter me?"

Lips pressed together, I lift both brows. "Um, not at the moment. I'd be okay with a little less of a good thing, if you know what I mean."

"Want me to look into a dick reduction?" he asks, smoothing one hand from my hip to my ribs and back again, a caress that is both relaxing and erotic.

"Would you?" I ask, breath coming faster as he cups my breast in his hand.

"Right now…" He glances down, watching as he rolls my nipple between his fingers, the need in his eyes making the waves of sensation dancing from my breast to pulse between my legs that much more intense. "Yes. I would. Anything to keep doing this. You feel so damned good, Violet. I'm sorry it isn't the same for you."

"It will be." I run my hands up his back to grip his shoulders, relishing the powerful feel of him beneath my fingers. "I still want you so much. I just need to take it slow."

"We can go as slow as you need, baby. I'm not in any rush," he says, illustrating his point by pulling out inch by careful inch, before sinking back inside with a gentleness that touches me in places not even his talented fingers could possibly reach.

"Yes," I whisper, holding his gaze as he stills inside me once more, the intimacy of the moment enough to make my throat tight. "Just like that. That's perfect."

"You're perfect," he says, kissing me as he glides out and then in and in and in until I'm completely filled with every glorious inch of him. "I could stay here for the rest of my life, inside you, just like this, and die a happy man."

"Oh God, Deacon." I shudder, hunger roaring to life inside of me again. "I want you so much. I can't remember ever wanting anyone this much."

"Then take me, gypsy. Show me how you like it. Tell me what you want."

Drunk on the smell of him and the feel of him and the rush of knowing he means every word—he really wants me to show him, to help him make our first time together incredible—I whisper, "Me on top. I want my hands on your chest."

"And I want my hands on yours," Deacon says as he wraps one big arm around me, holding me close as he rolls onto his back with his cock still deep inside me. "So that works out just fine."

"So fine," I agree, breath catching as he cups my breasts in his hands, rubbing his thumbs across my nipples as I begin to ride him. I try to go slow, to make sure the pain is really gone for good before I go too crazy, but that's not the way Deacon and I work. He's lightning, and I'm a field of dry summer grass, and this fire we make together isn't going out any time soon.

"Yes, oh yes," I gasp, nails digging into his pecs as my hips work faster, faster, until I slam into a wall of pleasure going ninety miles per hour.

But there's no pain on impact, only paradise, heaven, stars dripping down my face and spilling from my lips as I kiss him until I can't see anything but his bright blue eyes as he rolls on top of me and takes me there again.

I come apart, unraveling until there is nothing left of

daytime Violet. I'm all core, all heart, all the secret nighttime pieces only one man has ever seen.

I wasn't sure I'd ever feel this way with someone else ever again—like touching is about more than sex or even pleasure; that it's a language only the two of us understand. But here I am, with this man I barely know, with this person I was so sure wasn't my kind of sweet, and it is…so beautiful.

"So beautiful," I sob against his lips.

"So good," he murmurs, his voice tight. "So damned good, baby. Violet, I'm going to come. I'm going to come so fucking hard, I want you to come with me. Again. Come for me baby, please, I—"

His words are drowned out by the howl of a wild woman tumbling through an electric universe of bliss and light. He calls my name as he comes, his cock pulsing inside me, drawing out the spin until I'm weightless, breathless, lost and found on this desert island made of damp sheets.

"We got your sheets all sweaty," I say several long minutes later, still not quite myself, still not able to breathe without my chest hitching and echoes of pleasure shivering across my skin.

"I'm never going to wash them." Deacon wraps an arm around me, holding me close as we lie facing each other on our sides, my leg still wrapped around his waist and his softening erection lingering inside me.

"You want to sleep in my sweat forever?" I ask, grinning like a fool for some reason I can't quite put my finger on.

"Yes. If that's wrong, I don't want to be right."

My laugh becomes a hum of pleasure as he kisses me

again, long and slow. "We can always get them sweaty again, you know."

"Yeah? Even though we got off to a rough start?"

"It's not about the start, it's about the finish," I say, brushing his hair from his forehead. "And the finish was silver medal all the way."

"Not gold?" he asks, cupping my bottom in his hand and giving it a squeeze.

I smile. "Gotta give you a goal to shoot for. Don't want you to peak too early."

"I never peak too early, woman," he says, rolling on top of me with a wicked gleam in his eyes.

"Oh yeah?" I bite my bottom lip.

"Oh yeah," he confirms, and then he hooks my knees over his elbows and proves he's a man of his word.

CHAPTER 16

From the texts of Violet Boden and
Mina Smalls

Violet: We need to talk sexy times, woman. You've been holding out on me.

Mina: I have? About what? My therapist told me I'm too forthcoming about my sex life with my friends and should establish better boundaries.

Violet: Your therapist is a twit. You should have been telling me more, not less! Why didn't you warn me that losing my Divorce Virginity was going to hurt almost as much as losing my actual virginity?! I was totally unprepared!

Mina: OMG!! YOU DID IT! YOU GOT YOUR DV CARD PUNCHED! CONGRATULATIONS, LADY, WAY TO GO!

Violet: Thank you! It was amazing! After the hurting part, anyway, which he was very understanding about. But it would have been nice to know, going in, that pain was going to be involved.

Mina: Yeah, sadly, pussies are like goldfish. They have very short memories. If you don't throw a dick at them every once in a while, they freak out and forget what to do with it.

Violet: Apparently. Again, would have been nice to know twelve hours ago.

Mina: I'm so sorry! I was going to tell you! And give you tips to help things along. I just didn't want to scare you away when you were still in the fragile, afraid-to-jump-out-of-the-single-lady nest stage. You should have called me before the big event the way I told you to!

Violet: I didn't realize you were serious. I thought you just wanted in on the gossip.

Mina: Well, that, too. So give me the goods. Did he deliver in the sack? Does he know what to do with that love pistol in his pocket or is he shooting blanks?

Violet: Not sure what to do with that metaphor, but he's definitely shooting blanks. He's had a vasectomy, and we've both been tested, so we didn't have to worry about condoms. It was so nice! Grant refused to have a vasectomy, so I had to stay on birth control for years, even though it made me have migraines and itchy eyeballs.

Mina: That's great, honey, but I'm talking about orgasms. Were there orgasms?

Violet: So many orgasms. An embarrassing number of orgasms. His body is just…magical, Mina. I can't stop thinking about it. About his hands and his mouth and all his other parts… I'm sitting here at work, filling out mind-numbing order forms, and I can't quit smiling.

Mina: A magic man. Damn, it's been so long since I've had one of those.

Violet: I thought your last hot baby was the king of oral.

Mina: He was, but that was technical proficiency, not magic. Magic is a whole different animal.

Violet: That's what I feel like with him. An animal. Just wild and free and completely unselfconscious. After so many years with the same man in my bed, and then no one at all in my bed, I thought the first time with someone new would feel strange, awkward. But it didn't. Not even a little bit.

Mina: So how long until you see him again?

Violet: He mentioned grabbing a beer tonight, but we already spent Monday and Tuesday nights together, so maybe we should wait? Get a good night's sleep first?

Mina: Are you insane? Of course you should wait. You don't want to make it too easy for him, or he'll lose interest.

Violet: Ack, forget that. I'm too old to play stupid dating games. I like being with him, and he likes being with me. Why not just go with it? If he loses interest because I'm honest about enjoying his company, then he isn't the man I think he is and I won't be into him anymore, anyway.

Mina: Wow. So you aren't living in fear of losing access to the magic peen?

Violet: If he treats me badly, his peen won't be magic anymore. It will lose its power. Meanness breaks the peen spell every time.

Mina: You're so grounded in self-love, girl. A part of me wants to be like that.

Violet: LOL. And the other part?

Mina: It just wants to find a magic peen again, lock it in my basement, and never let it go.

Violet: Kidnapping is frowned upon in most dating circles, I hear.

Mina: Yeah. I'm trying to cut back. See you at Pilates later?

Violet: I can't. I've got to get home and get dinner on the table early, feed Adriana, watch some mindless TV, and lure her into a false sense of security so she won't be paying attention if I decide to sneak out the back door to meet Deacon later.

Mina: Why would you be sneaking out the back? She's eighteen, Violet. She's legally a full-grown person. She can feed herself. Better yet, have her make dinner for both of you while you're getting ready for your date. She should be thrilled that you're dating again, getting out there, living your life the way she's living hers.

Violet: It's cute that you think eighteen is full-grown. She's still a baby. And yes, she can feed herself, but I like cooking for her. And I like keeping my private business private. If this thing with Deacon gets serious, then I'll be open with my kids about it. But chances are it's just a fling that will burn bright and fizzle out fast. No need to get the kids involved until there's something to be involved in.

Mina: I hear you. And I get it. I guess. Though, I'm kind of glad I only have dogs to worry about. Though, they can get pretty territorial with unexpected visitors.

Violet: Nugget still humping your dates?

Mina: Every leg she can get her fluffy little paws around. It's embarrassing, but a good litmus test, too. If a guy's going to get angry at a tiny dust mop of a dog rubbing on his jeans, he's not my kind of crazy.

Violet: I like that…my kind of crazy. We're all crazy, aren't we?

Mina: Pretty much. But Pilates helps me stay out of the nuthouse. Are you sure you won't join me? I'm so much better at dragging my ass to the studio if I know someone is waiting there for me. I'll buy veggie burgers for you and Adriana after…

Violet: Tempting. Let me think about it and get back to you. I've got to run. Duty calls.

Mina: Later! And congratulations again. So happy for you, Vi, and wishing you a long and happy frolic with your magical peen.

CHAPTER 17

VIOLET

*M*agical peen... Good grief.

Tossing my phone back into my purse, I duck my chin, hiding my flushed cheeks behind my hair as I assure Virginia, "Be right with you, Ginny."

Mina is a mess, but this time around I'm in no position to judge. That magical peen and the man it's attached to are all I can think about. I was hoping that sealing the deal with Deacon might help me recover some of my lost focus, but so far, not-so-good. If anything, I'm even more lust-drunk than I was yesterday.

I'm so out of it, Virginia had to snap her fingers in front of my face to get my attention. It's ridiculous. *I'm* ridiculous.

But so happy and buzzed from last night I can't quit smiling.

"So what's up now?" I ask, pushing my chair away from my desk.

Ginny motions for me to follow her. "Come on. You

need to see." I trail her down the hallway, past the dog and cat kennels to the door leading out to the paddocks and the brush on the other side.

The brush that an older man in a khaki jacket and giant glasses is studying with a serious expression…

"Who is that?" I ask, startled by the sudden appearance of a stranger on the premises. We have our share of drop-in visitors, but they usually come in through the front door.

"That's the biologist the county sent over," Ginny says, fingers worrying at the fringe hanging off the edge of her rainbow-colored vest. "He won't talk to me, but maybe he'll talk to you."

"Why won't he talk to you?" I ask as I start down the steps.

"Well, I'm not sure if he would or not. I didn't try. I figured we should go in with the big guns first."

I arch a brow at her over my shoulder. "I'm the big guns?"

"No, you're the sex appeal," Virginia says with a grin. "You're practically glowing this morning, by the way. I'm guessing your date with Tristan's big brother went okay."

"Okay is a word you could use," I say, fighting a grin and failing. "Explosive and mind-blowing and paradigm-shifting are also accurate."

Ginny wrinkles her nose. "Sounds violent."

I sigh. "A little, but in the very best way."

"Makes me glad I'm off the shelf," she says with a sniff. "Life is unpredictable enough without introducing paradigm shifts into the mix. None of that for me, thank you very much. It's like when my mom saw her brother's ghost."

I skid to a stop by the paddock gate, turning to face her. "What?"

"My mom saw her brother's ghost," Ginny continues, as if the segue makes perfect sense. "But she wasn't the type of person who saw ghosts. Not even close. She was rational, logical. She played by the rules, and ghosts popping up in her garage while she was cleaning out storage boxes wasn't in her playbook. So she decided it didn't happen."

I squint at Ginny. "What? But it did happen, right? She really thinks she saw her brother's ghost?"

"Yeah. She did. He even spoke to her—asked her if she was going to be okay. They were really close. Twins who basically raised each other after their mom died and their dad started drinking."

I cock my head. "So, she saw and heard her twin brother. But she decided to believe that she didn't?"

"That's right. It would have been too much of a paradigm shift. So instead of believing it happened, she decided it *didn't* happen and went right on playing by her usual rules. And she lived a long and happy life until she died in her sleep last winter, just shy of her eighty-fifth birthday."

"I'm sorry for your loss," I say, frown deepening.

"It's all right. She was ready to go."

I nod, my brow still furrowed. "I just... I'm not sure what to make of that story. I guess, personally, I'd rather let go of the rules. Make room for the magic."

Ginny hugs her arms around her chest. "Magic is scary."

"I guess it can be. But it's also..."

"Magical?" Ginny supplies with a wry twist of her lips.

I laugh. "Yeah. That. And part of the reason we're here? To find the magic in the midst of all the other stuff?"

"I'm a former geologist, Violet. The closest I get to believing in magic is popping open a geode, and those crystals inside are there because of science, not magic."

"Well, Miss Science, that's a good reason you should talk to our visitor. You can put your scientific heads together and figure out whatever needs to be figured out much faster than I ever could."

"Oh no, I can't." Ginny shakes her head. "I'm not good with strangers."

"He's not a stranger, he's a brother from another mother." I hook my arm through hers, dragging her with me as I circle around the fence. "Scientists are your people, right? And I'm sure he's just here to tell us what we already know. That the salamanders are living in the old ground squirrel burrows and that removing the brush will cause erosion and destroy their habitat."

Virginia's chin retracts into her neck and her lips purse into a tight rosette, transforming her usually attractive features into something much less pleasant to look at. "Smile," I mutter through gritted teeth as we get closer to the man in the khaki vest. "He's not the enemy."

But Ginny doesn't smile and the man—when he glances up to see us approaching—doesn't smile, either. His eyes narrow, his shoulders roll back, and his chest puffs up as if he's preparing for a full-frontal attack, not a meeting with two employees of a not-for-profit animal shelter.

"Hi!" I wave with my most welcoming grin. "We just wanted to come say hi, see if you needed anything. A bottle of water, cup of coffee?"

The man shakes his head, his humorless expression not budging. "No thank you."

"Are you sure?" I ask. "It's no trouble at all. We're so glad you're here. Especially Ginny. She's the one who discovered the salamander colony last year."

The man's bushy gray brows lift as his focus shifts Ginny's way. "You classified the species? Do you have a background in herpetology?"

Ginny stands up straighter. "No, I'm a geologist. Former geologist, but I'm very familiar with the native flora and fauna. I've lived in Sonoma County all my life."

"I'm from San Diego," the man says, nodding. "But amphibians are my specialty. The state calls me in for almost all frog and salamander-related issues."

"It's nice that they have a specialist on call," Ginny says. "Unexpected, but nice."

The man makes a coughing sound. "Right? They finally realized that a garden-variety biologist isn't going to know a True Toad from an American Spadefoot."

Ginny visibly perks up, and I press my lips together, fighting a smile. Oh yeah, these two are going to get along like a house on fire. Heck, they might even find a little magic if they can get out of their own way.

But first, to get myself out of the way…

I smack my hand to my forehead with a sigh. "Oh no, I forgot to get the meds out this morning, and its time for the puppies' worm medicine." I touch a hand to Ginny's elbow. "Can you take over with…" I turn back to the herpetologist. "I'm sorry, what was your name?"

"Dr. Bartholomew Sutton," he says, pushing his glasses up his nose.

"Dr. Virginia Prentice," Ginny says without the slightest prodding from me. "But my friends call me Ginny."

"Nice to meet you, Ginny," Bart says, clearly having zero interest in learning my name. But that's just fine. Better than fine.

"Let me know if you two need anything from me," I say as I back away. "I'll be inside dosing up the pups."

I turn, heading back toward the shelter at a brisk walk, fingers crossing at my side. It's likely nothing will come from this meeting except some passionate discussion about the plight of endangered wildlife, but there's a chance a window may have cracked just wide enough to let some magic in.

But I don't want a cracked window. I want a door flung wide.

As soon as I get back to my desk, I pull out my cell and text Deacon—*On for tonight. Eight o'clock. Where do you want to meet?*

I get a response almost immediately, proving Deacon isn't worried about playing it cool, either. *How do you feel about karaoke?*

Laughing, I text, *I feel like it's crazy fun. As long as you don't care that I can't carry a tune in a bucket and that* Love Shack *is my go-to song.*

He texts back a crying with laughter emoji and,

Perfect. Let's meet at the Fainting Mongoose. I'll get there a little early and put our names in. The line can get pretty long.

I hesitate, chewing on my bottom lip, but finally type, *So you aren't bothered by the fact that I can't sing? As a musician, that doesn't drive you nuts?*

A beat later, my phone rings, making me jump and glance guiltily toward the main office, but Tristan and Zoey are currently elsewhere on the premises. And it's Deacon, so I can't help but answer. "Hey, I'm not supposed to be taking personal calls at work, you know."

"Tristan couldn't run that place without you. Your job is safe," Deacon says. Just the sound of his voice is enough to give me the chills. "And I need you to hear this from my lips. I love the sounds you make. All the sounds."

My cheeks, and other, less safe for work places, flush. "If you say so, but I'm warning you, my musical stylings are much less pleasing to the ear than my other sounds. I'm tone deaf. Completely."

"That's fine. Music is about appreciation, not perfection."

"That's what I tell my students about art. But I would be lying if I said the sight of a doo-doo vase doesn't make me cringe."

He chuckles. "A doo-doo vase?"

"A vase that collapses in on itself due to poor construction, making it look like an elephant took a dump on your wheel."

"I think I've made a few of those," he says, surprising me.

"You've worked with clay? When?"

"My entire flight was part of an art therapy initiative after our mission went bad in Afghanistan. We were part of a control group to see if art made emotional fallout easier to deal with. And it did. For most people. But I don't enjoy seeing things fall apart, even if it's just my tenth lousy attempt at a bud vase."

"And I don't enjoy torturing the ears of people who can hear what music is really supposed to sound like." I slide down to the floor, sitting cross-legged on the carpet as Luke, Tristan's dog, pads back into the room, headed for his bed in the corner. I have to get off this call and get back to work, but I can't resist asking one more time, "You promise hearing my ugly sounds won't make your soul cringe?"

"Nothing about you could make my soul cringe," he says in a husky whisper that makes all the hairs on my arms stand on end. "You make my soul happy. See you tonight, beautiful. I can't wait."

"Me, either. Bye." I hang up with a grin so wide Luke comes over to investigate, plopping down in my lap and demanding under-the-collar scratches until he's sure I'm okay.

"So much better than okay," I murmur into his soft fur. "So much better."

CHAPTER 18

VIOLET

I push through the door to the Fainting Mongoose a little after seven to find Deacon at a long table near the empty stage, surrounded by really good-looking women. And men, but it's the women—particularly the busty one hanging on Deacon's arm as she laughs at something a guy with a red beard is saying across the table—who catch my eye.

I consider backing out the way I came and texting Deacon to tell him I'm sick—I didn't realize this was a group date—but at that moment he turns on his stool, spotting me in the doorway.

His eyes light up, and that panty-melting grin spreads lazily across his full lips.

Instantly, I forget all about Busty, my singing-in-public jitters, and everything else.

God, I love that smile.

He slides off his stool, making his way through the crowded tables filled with people pouring over giant books full of karaoke songs. "Hey." He draws me in for one of his fiercely gentle hugs, the ones that make my chest feel like it's going to burst with delight. "Sorry about the date crashers. I got called into the firehouse today for what I thought was an emergency meeting, but it turned out to be a surprise party to congratulate me for landing the chief position."

My jaw drops. "You got it! Congratulations. That's amazing!"

He grins self-consciously. "Thanks. Yeah, I'm excited. It's going to be nice to feel useful again on a regular basis. And the volunteer crew are a great group of people." He grimaces. "Except for their inability to take a hint. I tried to explain that I had a date tonight, but somehow they took that as an invitation to join us for karaoke."

I squeeze his arm. "It's fine. I didn't expect to be singing badly in front of this many of your friends, but it'll be a good test."

"A test of what?" he asks.

"Of whether you're as okay with dating a woman who sings like a dying swan as you're pretending to be."

He laughs. "Stop it. You're not that bad."

"Oh, I am," I assure him. "I tried to sing lullabies to the girls when they were babies, but they'd end up crying their eyes out. Every time. Even infants can sense that something isn't right with all this." I gesture toward my throat and mouth.

"I like all that," Deacon says, wrapping an arm around my waist. "And I don't care if you're the worst singer in California, but you don't have to sing if you don't want to. I can swing by the DJ stand and take your name off the list."

I shake my head. "Nope. I'm getting up there. I don't back down from things that scare me. In fact…" I pull away from his embrace, digging into my purse until I find my phone. "I'm going to text my friend Mina and see if she wants to join us." I pull up Mina's contact and jab at the letters with my thumbs. "She has an incredible voice and is always telling me that anyone can learn to sing. This would be a great opportunity to show her just how wrong she is about that." I glance up at Deacon. "I mean, if that's okay with you? I figured since we're on a group date anyway…"

He nods. "Yeah. Text her. The more, the merrier."

I hit send, and we head for the table full of firefighters, already the loudest corner of the room. I don't know if all first responders love to party as much as these volunteers, but by the time Mina arrives an hour later, looking adorable in a pair of overalls and a black turtleneck, paired with a beret perched on her caramel-colored curls, things are getting downright rowdy. Deacon's friend Ferris is seeing how many empty bottles he can balance on his forehead, and his twin sister, Fiona, is trying to convince two of the other men to help her stand on her head while she takes an Angry Dragon shot.

"Wow, I had no idea karaoke was a contact sport," Mina says, laughing as she's jostled closer to the wall when Hoover leaps off the stage after his performance of "Paradise by the Dashboard Light," setting off a chain reaction in the rest of the crowd.

"I know." I squeeze her hand. "Are you going to be okay alone when I head up there? I'm probably after Deacon since he put our names in at the same time."

Mina flutters breezy fingers. "Please, woman. You know I go out all the time. I'm a professional at this point. Crowds don't scare me." She leans closer, adding beneath her breath. "And thank you for the invite to the hot firefighter convention, by the way. I mean, you've got the hottest one, of course," she says, motioning toward where Deacon is climbing the steps leading up to the stage, "but there are a few I wouldn't kick out of bed for eating crackers. And I don't see wedding rings."

I nudge her ribs with my elbow. "Go for it girl. If you can get a word in edgewise." I cast a pointed look at Busty, who I now know is named Karen, but who will always be Busty McChattykins to me. The woman hasn't stopped talking since I sat down, though, she did stop touching Deacon every five seconds, which was nice.

Mina smirks. "Don't worry about me. I'll separate one from the herd and have him all to myself by the time you're finished delighting us all with the gift of song."

I snort. "You're going to be so deeply disillusioned."

Mina's lips part, but her reply is drowned out by an opening guitar solo. I recognize the intro to "More than a Feeling" and a delighted grin dances across my face.

"Does he know this is your favorite song?" Mina asks, raising her voice to be heard over the music.

"I don't know. I did mention it once. We were on our way back from lunch on our first date, and it came on the radio." I beam up at Deacon, who's smiling down at me with a knowing expression that makes it clear this isn't a coincidence.

"Oh man, this guy has game. We'll have to keep an eye on him," Mina grumbles, but she's smiling, too, a smile that stretches wider as Deacon begins to sing in a rich, resonant voice that makes the hair on my arms stand on end.

Within the first few notes, it's obvious that he's going to be amazing. But by the time he gets to the chorus, belting it out with an easy confidence that turns my bones to jelly, it's clear he's got a gift, something precious I feel so lucky to be here to appreciate. Every time his gaze connects with mine, it sends an electric shock through my system. By the time he finishes, I'm vibrating at a completely different frequency than I was before.

All I want to do is rush across the room, throw my arms around him, and devour the sexy mouth that made all those beautiful sounds.

But the DJ is calling my name.

I take a deep breath and start through the crowd, feeling sorry for all the innocent, unsuspecting ears I pass on my way to the stage. They have no idea what's about to happen to them, and though I'll try to warn them, I already know they aren't going to listen. People never do, assuming it can't possibly be *that* bad.

It's a mistake they live to regret.

"You might want to step outside for a breath of fresh air until I'm finished, guys," I say as I take the mic, wrapping my fingers around the still-warm metal as I move into the spotlight. "Seriously. This is going to hurt you more than it hurts me."

"You've got this, gorgeous," Deacon calls out, giving me two thumbs-up from near the front of the crowd as the opening strains of "Love Shack" fill the air.

I smile down at him with a shake of my head.

"You're about to eat those words, baby. And wish you'd brought earplugs."

The room ripples with laughter. Deacon laughs, too, and keeps laughing—softly, hiding his shit-eating grin behind his hand—as I open my mouth and suffering animal sounds come out.

Almost instantly, the room goes quiet, horror and disbelief creeping into the expressions of everyone in attendance, except Deacon. His shoulders simply continue to shake, proving he finds my tone-deafness absolutely hysterical. By the time I'm halfway through the song, I'm laughing, too, which doesn't make my singing any better, but doesn't make it worse, either—nothing could do that.

But once people see that I'm having fun at my own expense, they start smiling, too. And then Mina starts to sing along, followed by the rest of the volunteer department and the patrons near the stage. Soon, the entire bar is howling "Love Shack, baby!" and dancing in spaces between the tables, covering my caterwauling with the sweet sound of a hundred voices mixing together in song.

I finish the last note and thrust both arms into the air in Victory as cheers fill the bar. They're even louder than the applause after Deacon finished his number, and I can't stop grinning as I slip the mic back into the stand.

I leave the stage, high-fiving the hands held up in my path, and when I reach Deacon, he scoops me into his arms, hugging me so hard my feet leave the ground as he growls into my ear, "You're a badass, Violet Boden."

I giggle as I pull back to look into his eyes. "I didn't scare you off?"

He shakes his head. "No way. I'm even crazier about you than I was before. You're fearless, woman, and it's sexy as hell."

I bite my bottom lip. "Not as sexy as that incredible voice of yours. I want you to sing to me. In my bed. While we're naked. Right now."

His eyes flash. "I'll pay the bill and meet you outside. Five minutes."

I say goodbye to Mina and the rest of the fire crew and make a beeline for the door.

And for the first time, we go to my place, sneaking up the stairs only to find that Adriana isn't at home studying like she promised. But not even my wayward teen can cool my hunger to get naked with this man.

"I'm going to sew a tracking device into her coat," I murmur against Deacon's lips as we drift toward my room.

"I'll help you. I know where we can get one for cheap."

"I was kidding," I say. "Mostly. But thank you. I shouldn't be too worried, though, right? She'll be okay. She's still getting great grades, and I never smell alcohol on her breath. She could just be at Georgia's studying."

"She could be. Whatever she's up to, she's a smart kid," he says. "She's going to be fine. And so are you, if I have anything to say about it."

"You always make me feel fine." I kiss him as I add, "So much better than fine."

And he does. For hours, until we hear Addie tiptoe

in around midnight, and we both agree it's time to get some rest.

I sleep better than I have in months, tucked into the small-spoon position with this man I'm beginning to think might be perfect for me, after all.

CHAPTER 19

From the texts of Tristan Hunter and
Deacon Hunter

Tristan: Hey! I just got a call from Dad, sounds like congratulations are in order!

Deacon: Thanks. Yeah, I got the news yesterday. I start full-time next week. Two days on, three days off, with on-call hours split between me and the former chief, who's going to stay on part-time until we get someone trained to take his place.

Tristan: I'm not talking about the job—though, that's great and I'm happy for you—I'm talking about the fact that you didn't go home last night. Violet let you stay over at her place, huh? Must be getting serious.

Deacon: Or I could have been passed out in the alley

behind the karaoke joint. Or in a car accident. Or have decided to make a last-minute trip to Vegas.

Tristan: Obviously none of these things are true. You're in her bed right now, aren't you?

Deacon: No comment.

Tristan: Ha! Knew it. Good for you, brother. Tell her she can take off today if she wants. There's not much on the schedule, just a few adoptions and another visit from the herpetologist. He's saying it's going to take at least a month for him to work up his final report and recommendations, by the way. So I'll have plenty of time to find someone else to take care of brush removal when the time comes, since you're going to be busy.

Deacon: I won't be too busy. When you're ready to deal with it, I'll be there. I'd rather supervise the process myself. There are a lot of people I care about at that shelter. I want to make sure you're all safe.
And Violet says thank you.
She could use a day off to ride her kid's ass for sneaking out last night.

Tristan: Ha. Knew you were still in bed with her.

Deacon: Shut up.

Tristan: Wish her good luck with Adriana, and be sure to tell her all the stories about Rafe and Dylan when they were teens. They made lying and sneaking around

153

their full-time job, and both of them turned out just fine.

Deacon: Will do. But I'll leave out the part where Rafe almost got shot sneaking into his girlfriend's window in the middle of the night.

Tristan: Yeah, do that. I'm sure Adriana has more sense than to break into the home of a man whose property is covered with "No Trespassing, Violators Will Be Shot, Survivors Will Be Shot Again" signs.

Deacon: She does seem like a smart kid. I just wish she wasn't upsetting Violet so much and that there was something I could do to help.

Tristan: Judging from the smile on Violet's face the past few days, I'd say you're doing your part. She seems happy. So do you.

Deacon: I am. She's special. I don't know how long she'll be able to put up with me, but I'm sure as hell enjoying it while it lasts.

Tristan: I wouldn't worry about how long it's going to last. I've got a feeling about you two.

Deacon: Don't jinx it.

Tristan: You can't jinx love. Violet told me that. And she's a smart woman, especially about this kind of thing.

Deacon: She is. One of the smartest I've ever met. Talk to you later. I'm going to go make her pancakes, to show her how much I appreciate sleepover privileges.

Tristan: Excellent call.

Deacon: I may be rusty, baby brother, but I'm no fool. Especially when it comes to people I'd like to keep in my life for the foreseeable future.

CHAPTER 20

VIOLET

*T*ime flies when you're having fun.

And when you're falling in love...

Well, it flashes by at the speed of light.

I blink, and November is winding to a close, ushered out with Thanksgiving at my mom's place with the girls and a turkey sandwich picnic with Deacon the day after, shared around the fire pit behind my house with a bottle of Chardonnay and two miniature pumpkin pies from his stash of leftovers. And though I'd never tell my mother or any of the other guests at her holiday feast, my belated Thanksgiving with Deacon is my favorite part of the long weekend.

Thanksgiving is all about gratitude, and of all the things I'm thankful for this year, Deacon is quickly becoming one of my top two, right up there with the health of my babies and all the other people I love.

He just makes me so...happy. In a way I didn't think I'd ever be happy again.

And then December arrives with a freak cold snap,

and the pipes in my ancient basement freeze and burst, flooding the southeast corner and taking out my washer and dryer while they're at it. Deacon and his new employees from the volunteer fire department are on the scene within the hour. Even though it's a Sunday and they all just got off an all-night shift, and I'm sure the last thing they want to do on the first frigid day of the year is to help pump water out of a basement.

But they do. They pump and scrub and set up fans with smiles on their faces. I'm sure part of that is due to the spiked hot cocoa I keep bringing down on trays throughout the afternoon, but the major reason is the man who gathers me into his arms when the mess is finally under control and promises he knows a guy who sells appliances cheap and owes him a favor.

Deacon inspires the people he leads, and he's clearly a perfect fit for his new job as captain of the volunteer department. And though I miss the time when he only worked a few afternoons a week, I'm so proud of him.

"You're a good boss," I whisper, patting his chest with one hand as I wave goodbye to his coworkers with the other.

"I'm not sure Ferris and Fiona would agree," he says with a chuckle. "They were looking forward to watching football all day. But spiked hot chocolate seems to have softened the blow. Hopefully they won't have tacks waiting in my chair when I get there on Wednesday."

I hum happily as I lean my cheek against his chest. "That's right. It's the start of your weekend. What's on your wish list for your time off?"

"Naps." He yawns. "Lots of naps."

"Old man," I tease, hugging him closer.

"So old. And tired. So old and tired, I may need help getting into bed, Vi."

I tilt my head back, shooting him a wry smile. "Is that right?"

He nods, his brow furrowed pitifully. "It is."

"You poor thing, let me help you upstairs. We'll get you tucked in, and you can sleep as long as it takes to recover your strength. I'll bring you hot water bottles and cups of tea until you're right as rain."

"A hot water bottle wasn't what I had in mind." His hand drops to cup my ass through my jeans, and we shut the door and head up the stairs. "I was thinking of a hot brunette. One with really long hair I like to wrap my hands up in while I'm fucking her from behind."

"Shush!" I turn on the steps, giving him a wide-eyed look as I press my finger to my lips and add in a whisper, "Adriana is upstairs in her room studying for the driver's test she's already failed three times."

He grimaces, casting a worried glance over my shoulder. "Shit. Do you think she heard? I didn't think she was here. I haven't seen her since before lunch."

I frown. "Not this again. She should be here. She didn't tell me she was leaving." I start back up the stairs and moving left down the hall until I get to Addie's room. "Addie, honey, would you mind going to the store for me in a bit? Just the corner market. We need bread and black beans and almond coffee creamer."

I pause, waiting for a response that doesn't come. "Addie? Are you asleep?" I wait another beat before reaching for the handle and turning, opening the door to reveal Addie's empty bed, empty desk, and empty ratty old couch she insisted on dragging home from a flea market two years ago.

Deacon grunts behind me, and I sigh.

"You were right. I guess I should have invested in a tracking device, after all. But I was hoping we were done with this. She hasn't snuck out without telling me where she was going in weeks."

"That you know of," Deacon says. And though I don't like to admit it, he's right.

"What am I going to do?" I run a hand through my hair, suddenly feeling all the hours of running drinks and equipment up and down the basement stairs. "I mean, she seems fine, so I don't want to worry, but every mom instinct I've got is screaming that something isn't right. That she needs my help but is too afraid to ask for some reason."

Deacon places a comforting hand on my back. "Then let's put our heads together and come up with a plan. Figure out what she's up to."

I turn to him, overcome with a sudden rush of gratitude so powerful I can't help throwing my arms around his waist and hugging him tight. "Thank you," I murmur against the soft fabric of his sweatshirt.

"Don't thank me yet," he says, returning the embrace. "We don't have a plan, and I'm too tired to think of one right now. I've been up for over twenty-four hours, and I may have had one too many shots of Schnapps in my cocoa."

I take his hand, smiling as I lead him down the hall. "We don't need a plan right now. Just knowing I've got a partner in surveillance is enough for today. And I'm happy to just take a nap with you if you're too tired for other kinds of fun."

"I'm never too tired for other kinds of fun," he says, shutting the door to my bedroom and locking it behind us.

As always, he's a man of his word.

CHAPTER 21

From the texts of Deacon Hunter and
Violet Boden

Deacon: How's your Thursday, sexy? Missed not having you in my bed last night.

Violet: Me, too. I was freezing. I've gotten used to having a furnace person with me in between the sheets.

Deacon: Your furnace will be back in operation soon. I'm off at midnight. Is operation Addie Track still a go for tomorrow?

Violet: I think so… She's definitely still planning on going out. It's not wrong to spy on her, is it? Am I a terrible mother who's betraying the mother-daughter trust bond? Should I be sent to the corner for a timeout?

Deacon: No, you're a good mother who's concerned that your daughter's involved with someone who isn't right for her. You're an open-minded person with a big heart —it's not like you're going to disapprove of Adriana's choice of partner for some superficial reason. If she's hiding this guy from you, then there's probably something to hide.

Violet: That's what I think! But it's good to hear it from someone else. I'm sure her dad would agree, too, but I don't want to tell him anything just yet. No need to worry him until I'm sure what's going on. He tends to fly off the handle when it comes to the kids. If he had his way, the girls would all be locked away in a tower until they're thirty.

Deacon: If I had girls, I'm sure I'd be the same way. My boys are gentlemen, but I know most men their age aren't.

Violet: Thank you for raising two good ones. It's nice to know that there are at least a couple out there. But it does raise the question—what do we do when we find out Adriana's dating one of the bad ones? I mean, legally she's an adult and can date whomever she chooses.

Deacon: She's living under your roof, eating your food, sleeping in a room you pay to heat. Until those things aren't true, she's still a kid and subject to the rules of her mother's house.

Violet: I can't threaten her with homelessness if she doesn't break up with this jerk, Deacon. That's too heartless. Besides, knowing Adriana, that would only make her want this guy more. She's stubborn.

Deacon: Like her mother?

Violet: Worse. Much worse. My mind is relatively open and can be changed. Occasionally.

Deacon: A fact I'm grateful for every time I kiss you…

Violet: Oh, God, don't talk about kissing. I'm dying for one, and it hasn't even been two full days yet.

Deacon: I could come over when I get off work. Or you could come here…

Violet: I can't. I'm at Adriana's track meet, and afterward, I'm taking her and her friends for pizza and a late movie. They don't have school tomorrow, and none of them have their driver's license except Georgia, and she's so traumatized after hitting Dash that she's been bussing it along with the rest of them.

Deacon: How is Dash?

Violet: Healing up, slowly but surely. If all goes well, Dr. Moshin says he should be ready to be put up for adoption in another week or two.

Deacon: And you're actually going to let that happen?

Violet: I have to. He's a sweetheart, but I already have four cats, three birds, two rats my oldest swears she's going to take to her dorm, but never does, and an aquarium full of fish. I've got my hands full.

Deacon: But you don't have a dog. Dogs are the best. A dog's devotion never falters. If there's one thing you can trust in the world, it's a dog's love.

Violet: I used to have a dog. Two, actually. Grant took Frankie and Penelope with him when he moved out.

Deacon: Asshole.

Violet: It's okay. Now they live with Tracey, love her dearly, and are very happy. That's the other great thing about dogs—they bloom where they're planted. If the person they used to love isn't around, they'll find someone else to adore and be just as happy as they were before.

Deacon: If we broke up, I would never take the dogs and leave you with nothing but a pack of moody cats.

Violet: My cats aren't moody! Pukey, sometimes, but not moody.

Deacon: Still…they're cats.

Violet: True. They are. And I appreciate the promise, though, I don't think we have to worry about that just yet. In order to break up, we'd have to officially be together.

Deacon: Then let's officially be together.

Violet: We've only been dating for six weeks. You could have a secret family in Peoria for all I know.

Deacon: Do you think I have a secret family? And where is Peoria? Illinois?

Violet: I'm not sure. And no, I don't think you have a secret family. I think you're honest, almost to a fault. It's one of the things I really like about you.

Deacon: I really like that about you, too. And I don't need more time to know I want more time. I'm into you, Violet Boden. Way into you. But if you're not ready to put a label on this, it's okay. I can wait.

Violet: I'm way into you, too. I mean, spending two days apart feels like it's causing lasting damage. I'd say I'm pretty hooked.

Deacon: Then be my girlfriend. Let's make it official.

Violet: Okay.

Deacon: Not the show of enthusiasm I would have liked, but I'll take it.

Violet: LOL. Sorry! I am enthusiastic. I'm smiling so

hard right now the people in the stands around me are starting to look at me funny. I'm goofy happy to be your girlfriend. Truly.

Deacon: Good. I like you goofy happy. I can't wait to see you again, baby.

Violet: Me, either. Tomorrow can't come fast enough. Adriana said she was leaving around noon, by the way.

Deacon: Then I'll be there by eleven. In case she heads out early.

Violet: Or you could come over at ten, and we could go grab brunch at the diner first. I mean, who knows where she's going? It could end up being a long day. We'll want to be sure we start with a hearty breakfast.

Deacon: True. And sometimes there's a line for brunch on Fridays. Maybe I should get there at nine, just in case.

Violet: Or eight. And we could linger over coffee…

Deacon: I like the way you think, woman. And I love the way you taste. Are you sure I can't come over? I'll make it worth your while…

Violet: You always do, which reminds me of a question I've wanted to ask you.

Deacon: Shoot. You know I'm an open book.

Violet: How on earth did you manage to stay single for so long? A catch like you?

Deacon: You didn't think I was such a catch when we first met.

Violet: Yeah, well you grew on me. A lot. Surely, sometime in the past twelve years, there was another woman who could put up with your pretty face and lovely muscles and gorgeous singing voice and how obnoxiously helpful and generous you are.

Deacon: There were a couple. But in my gut, I knew those relationships wouldn't work long term. As a wise woman I know once said, I'd rather be alone than be with someone who doesn't check my boxes.

Violet: And what are your boxes, Mr. Hunter?

Deacon: I'd rather tell you in person, Ms. Boden, while checking your boxes until you scream my name.

Violet: Addie and her friends are sleeping at my place. So that's a hard no on the screaming.

Deacon: Then why don't I pick you up after you get home from the movie, and we can come back here? The twins are home for the weekend, but they stay in the guest cottage, and Dad's over at Sophie's, so it'll be just the two of us in the main house.

Violet: I like just the two of us... And the girls will be

fine on their own. But I have to be back at my place by seven tomorrow to make breakfast. I promised them mushroom and feta omelets.

Deacon: Done.

Violet: Perfect. *winking emoji* See you soon.

Deacon: Not soon enough.

CHAPTER 22

VIOLET

I love spending time with my kids. Every age and every stage has been precious—even the terrible toddler years and the equally trying interpersonal obstacle course that is parenting teenagers. I wouldn't trade a moment of the time I've spent watching movies or riding bikes or hunting through the bargain bins at the thrift store with my girls for eternal life and a bucket full of money.

But tonight my mind isn't with Addie and her friends.

I try to focus on the rapid-fire gossip ricocheting through the car as I pull out of the pizza parlor parking lot and head for the movies, but I can't seem to make sense of the names or backstories or who's cheating on who with whose ex-best-friend from Cloverdale.

I usually enjoy this window into Addie's world, but tonight my thoughts aren't in this car. They're in Mercyville with the man I can't get out of my head.

With my newly official boyfriend…

I have a *boyfriend* for the first time since I was Addie's age. And it's wonderful. Amazing. So much better than I remember.

Deacon is so special, and this thing we've found is so much more intense than anything I've felt before, even in the beginning with Grant, when I was so starry-eyed I tripped over my own feet in my hurry to fall in love.

But not even Grant made me burn like this, want like this, *long* for him like this. And it isn't just physical longing anymore. It hasn't been for weeks. It's Deacon's smile, his laugh, the way he puts my needs first and goes out of his way to memorize my favorite things, and how he holds me like he never wants to let me go.

God, I've got it so bad—so bad I know I won't be able to keep it to myself much longer.

"Earth to Mom," Addie says from the back seat, in a tone that makes me think it isn't the first time she's said my name. "Are you okay?"

"Fine." I force a smile, meeting her gaze in the rearview mirror. "Just thinking about everything I need to get done tomorrow."

"You missed the turn into the parking garage," Addie says, clearly not convinced that I haven't finally gone senile, the way she's been anticipating for years.

I blink, laughing uncomfortably as I realize I'm nearly to the mall "Sorry. Woolgathering. Good thing we're early."

Turning the car around, I force myself to focus on the road, the conversation, the way Addie goes weirdly quiet when Georgia mentions going camping for spring break—she usually loves camping—but my thoughts keep coming back to Deacon.

Long before I climb into his truck after getting the girls settled in Adriana's room with strict orders not to leave until I get back tomorrow morning unless the house is on fire, I'm already with Deacon in spirit.

In heart and soul.

"And finally in body," I sigh, leaning across the cab for a kiss.

"What's that about your fine body?" he murmurs against my lips.

"It's happy to be with you again."

"Mine, too. I missed you so much," he says, shifting into drive before bringing his hand back to rest on my thigh. "That's one of my boxes. That life has to feel better with the person I'm with than it does alone."

I turn, studying him as he drives, the streetlights illuminating his strong profile. "So I pass the better life test?"

"You make everything better," he says, casting a soft glance my way. "Me, included."

My chest squeezes tight, and my stomach flips in a way I never expected it to flip again. But it turns out falling in love isn't only for the young or naïve. It's for everyone, at every age, from the most wide-open heart to the most jaded soul wandering the earth and secretly hoping there's someone out there made just for them.

"I want to hear more about your boxes," I whisper.

"I want to get you naked as soon as possible."

"Then you'd better talk fast. It's only a ten-minute drive, buddy."

With a smile and a deep breath, he confesses all his secrets, as if they aren't secrets at all. As if he's never considered hiding any of the things he unravels in the dark as we zip through the still night toward the river.

But I know better. Deacon is fiercely private. The fact that his walls have come down for me is special. The fact that they've come down so fast I suspect is unprecedented, a hunch he confirms when he says, "I've never told anyone most of those things. Not even my ex-wife when we were in counseling. But, with you, I don't feel like I have to hide or pretend like I've got everything under control." He laughs, the sound so soft it's almost lost beneath the rumble of gravel as he turns into his driveway. "Sometimes, I think you like me better when I'm struggling to figure shit out."

I grin as I brush his increasingly long hair behind his ear. "Sometimes, I do. Struggling means you're growing, and growing is sexy."

"I'm definitely growing," he says, his fingers sliding higher on my thigh.

"You're shameless," I say, my giggle turning to a sigh as his hand settles firmly between my legs. "It's one of the things I love about you."

He somehow manages to shift the truck into park and turn off the ignition without moving his right hand, and then his lips are on mine. "I love everything about you."

"Lies," I whisper, my pulse beating fast in my throat. "Sometimes I drive you crazy."

"Which I also love. You keep me on my toes." His hand skims up to my waist as he pulls back to meet my eyes in the dim glow of the light shining from the barn roof. "What I'm trying to say is..." His breath rushes out. "Something I haven't said in a long time."

I nod, breath held, heart racing. "It hasn't been quite as long for me, but it's still a scary thing to say."

"Only if the other person doesn't feel the same way," he says. "But it's okay. If you're not there yet, I can wait, Vi. There's no pressure."

"Are you going to say it?" I whisper. "Or wait until I have a heart attack first?"

His lips quirk. "I do know mouth-to-mouth. But I don't want to give you a heart attack. I love you too much. I want to keep you and your heart in good working order."

Champagne bubbles of happiness exploding in my bloodstream, I wrap my arms around his neck, hugging him tight. "I love you and your heart, too."

"As much as you love my cock?"

I draw away, feigning serious consideration. "Nearly. Very nearly."

"Who's shameless now?" He laughs and tickles me until I spill out of the truck to escape his fingers.

But I let him catch me on the porch, on the stairs, on the landing outside his bedroom before we sway inside and close the door, where we prove just how in love we are with every sweet and sexy kiss.

CHAPTER 23

DEACON

The only thing better than going to sleep with Violet in my arms is waking up to find her still there.

Though, I confess I'd take being awoken by the sun peeking in through the curtains over the high-pitched yapping sound blaring from Violet's phone.

"Oh my fuh, wha?" She gropes her way across the sheets, eyes still closed as she fumbles for the phone on the bedside table. I squint her way, fighting a groan as I see the time.

Four forty-five a.m. A call at this time can only mean one thing—someone's in trouble. I just hope it isn't a kid. Or serious. Or both.

I sit up, reaching for the T-shirt and jeans Violet tossed to the floor when she ripped them off of me last night, intending to get dressed and ready to drive us wherever we need to go. I'm definitely coming with her, even if she fights me about it. No way I'm letting her face an emergency alone with only a few hours of sleep under her belt. We didn't get to bed until after one in the morning.

Well, we got to bed…

Just not to sleep.

"Woah, woah, slow down, Ginny," Violet says, swinging her legs over the side of the bed as she sits up. "What's going on?" Her fingers abruptly freeze, mid-eye-rub. "What? Say that again."

Her eyes go wide as they shift my way with a smile that makes me hope this isn't a Code Red situation, after all. "Good for you, woman. That's wonderful, I was hoping you two would hit it off but I never…" Violet trails off, wincing at something Virginia is saying on the other end of the line. "Yeah, I know. That happens apparently. The next time shouldn't be painful at all. Uh-huh. Yes. Honestly." She scoots back into bed, covering her tempting bare legs with the blankets and propping up against the headboard, motioning for me to join her.

I hold up a finger and then jab a thumb toward the bathroom, and she smiles again, nodding as she asks Ginny, "So is that the bad news? You said you had good news and bad."

I head for the bathroom, use the facilities, wash my hands, and give my teeth a quick brush on the off chance Violet is up for letting me kiss her back to sleep for an early morning power nap. But when I return, she's pacing the rug in front of the bed with a thoughtful expression, and I know we're not headed back to bed any time soon.

"What's up?" I ask, pushing aside my disappointment.

"The tiger salamanders," she says, curling a lock of hair around her finger the way she does when she's thinking or worried or both. "Looks like they might not be tiger salamanders. That's what prompted the early morning call. Ginny's freaking out, worried that you and Tristan are going to kill them because they're not the endangered kind of salamanders."

"I'm not planning on killing anything." I sit down in the wingback chair near the window, threading my hands together. "I'm sure Tristan's not, either, but ultimately it's his call. Hopefully we can find a compromise. But something does need to be done about the brush. It's a fire hazard, and you know how deadly the wildfires have been the past few years."

"I know, I just—" She's cut off by a crashing sound from outside. "What the hell was that?"

"Probably raccoons in the garbage again," I say, turning to pull the curtains away from the window. "The boys always forget to put the rocks back on top of the lids when they take the trash out."

But when my eyes adjust to the dim light pooling around the garage from the barn lamp, I don't see a trash bandit pawing through last night's leftovers.

I see a girl in a sock cap with a long braid trailing from beneath it replacing the can in its upright position, while one of the twins shoves the spilled trash bags back inside. At first, I'm not sure if it's Jacob or Blake, but then he laughs, and I can tell from the way his shoulders shake that it's Jacob.

Only that's not Raney, his girlfriend of nearly three years, who he's pulling into his arms and kissing tenderly on the forehead. This is someone new, a girl he hasn't told me jack shit about, and we haven't discussed whether it's kosher to have girls for overnight visits. I know my dad couldn't care less who's shacking up on his property, but I'm not sure I'm ready to start running into my twenty-year-old sons' fuck buddies every time I pop over to have dinner or play Xbox with the kids.

Not to mention the fact that the two tiny bedrooms in the guesthouse are separated by an inch-thick piece of plywood Dad threw up when the kids decided they wanted separate spaces a few years ago. Out of respect for Blake in the other room, who I'm sure isn't thrilled about hearing every creak and moan coming from his brother's bed, Jacob should have discussed this with the family first.

"What's going on?" Violet asks, coming up behind me.

"Looks like Jacob decided to bring a lady friend home without telling me about it," I whisper, on the off chance my voice might carry through the glass to the couple now kissing below.

"Guess it runs in the family," Violet says with a laugh that becomes a swiftly indrawn breath as she leans down to peer out the window. "Holy shit..." Bracing one hand on my shoulder, she jabs a finger at the pool of light. "That's Adriana. That's my daughter."

CHAPTER 24

VIOLET

*M*y daughter is not at home in bed where she promised me she would be. My daughter is running around Sonoma County at five in the morning, making out with Deacon's son right under my nose.

Literally.

If I threw open the window and leaned out, I'd be able to drop a piano on her lying, sneaking head.

"What are we going to do about this?" I hiss, watching in horror as Jacob wraps Adriana's long braid around his hand with a possessiveness that's way too familiar. Did he learn that move from his dad? Do fathers and sons exchange tips like that? Most importantly, did Deacon have any idea this was going on?

I cut my gaze sharply his way. "You didn't know, did you?"

Brow furrowed, Deacon shakes his head. "No. Of course not. Are you sure it's her? I haven't seen her face, it could be another—"

"I'm sure," I say, shifting my attention back to the increasingly steamy scene below. "I know my daughter. That's her hair, her shoulders, her skinny little ass getting fondled through her jeans."

Jacob now has Addie's bottom in both of his hands, pulling her closer as she wraps her arms tight around his neck and kisses him like his lips are made of those churro chips she couldn't get enough of last summer. If someone doesn't throw a bucket of water on them soon, they'll be banging against the side of the barn before we know it.

"Get your clothes on." Deacon stands, plucking his sweater from the floor near the bed. "We're going down there."

I hesitate, torn between irritation that he's jumped straight to giving orders, skipping the discussion part of the decision-making process, and relief that someone's taking charge. But that's *my* daughter out there, and I'm the one in charge of deciding what's best for her. I have to make this call with a level head, no matter how much I want to bury it in the sand and let someone else decide how to handle this sticky situation.

"Wait." I lift my hands, stepping in front of Deacon as he starts for the door. "Let's think this through."

"I don't need to think it through," he says. "I need to ask my son why he thinks it's okay to keep things from me and run around with a girl who's still in high school."

"And I want to swat his hands off her butt with a willow switch, drag her home by her ear, and lock her in her room for the next decade. But that's not going to help us move toward an adult relationship with either one of them."

"She's not an adult," Deacon says, thrusting an arm toward the door. "Hell, he's barely an adult, but she's definitely still too young for him. He should know better."

"She's eighteen, and only six months from graduation," I find myself saying, even as I wonder who popped the words into my mouth. "I wish she hadn't lied to me, but she's of legal age, and maybe there's a reasonable explanation for all this. Maybe they knew that you and I were dating and she didn't want to—"

"You said Adriana started sneaking months ago, way before we were ever a thing," he cuts in. "Unless you think she was sneaking around with someone else before moving in on Jake."

My brows shoot up so fast I stumble back a step. "Woah. Hold up a second. That sounded an awful lot like you were slut-shaming my daughter."

Deacon's shoulders creep closer to his ears. "Of course I wasn't. But until now, Jacob was with the same girl for years. He's a loyal kid. A loving kid."

"And now he's what? Slutting it up with my wild daughter?"

"No!" He exhales, fingers spreading wide in front of him. "Let's just go talk to them. See what's going on before they leave."

"I think we should let them go," I say, crossing my arms. "We're both surprised and upset. We should wait until the shock's worn off. We don't want—"

"I want to talk to my son. And I'm going to. Now.

You can decide how you want to handle things with Adriana," he says, starting for the door.

For a moment, I consider trying to block his path again, but I've known Deacon long enough to recognize his "unstoppable force" face. He's going down there, no matter what I have to say about it.

Now I just have to decide if I'm going, too.

"Shit, shit, shit," I mutter as I pull on my dress and sweater from last night and hurry after him. I pad down the steps, shove my feet into my clogs, and push through the back door into the chilly December morning to find Deacon already in mid-lecture and the kids with their backs pressed against the weathered siding of the guest house. Jacob looks mortified and Adriana so utterly shocked that it's immediately clear to me that she had no idea my Deacon was her Jacob's dad.

My Deacon…

He might not be my Deacon after tonight. How can I keep dating a man who plows over me like a steamroller every time his judgment call clashes with mine? Decisions need to be made as a team, especially decisions with serious consequences like this one. Jacob and Adriana care about each other—a lot. That's immediately evident, too. Even now, with his dad reading him the riot act, Jacob holds tight to Addie's hand, his thumb brushing back and forth across her knuckles, and Addie is clinging to his arm like it's her lifeline in a world gone mad.

She trusts him, maybe even loves him, I realize as her eyes begin to shine with unshed tears and her bottom lip quivers. She's about to fall apart, and Deacon is still yelling at Jacob, something about respect for his brother's space that is completely irrelevant to the matter at hand.

"That's enough," I say, stepping off the porch and starting across the dry grass.

Adriana's gaze immediately shifts my way, her eyes going even wider with a mix of relief and fear that makes my heart twist in my chest. "Mom? What are you doing here?"

"That's a question we'd like you two to answer first," Deacon says. "We're adults who pay our own bills. We don't have to explain our behavior."

"Take a breath, Deacon," I say, motioning toward the two clearly distraught almost-adults in front of us. "They're upset. We're upset. Let's all calm down. Why don't I make us some tea, and we can go inside where it's warm and sort this out in our inside voices?"

"Dad doesn't have an inside voice when he's mad," Jacob says, his resentment clear. "He goes into drill sergeant mode, and that's it, no one else can get a word in edgewise."

"Watch it," Deacon says softly. "I won't be disrespected in my own house."

"I'm not disrespecting you. I'm trying to explain, but you won't listen," Jacob says. "And Blake isn't even here, so there's no reason to worry about him being bothered by Addie and me. He's over at Ms. Baxter's house. They've been banging like bunnies since last summer, and she's ten years older than he is. If you want to have a rage stroke about something, do it about that."

"At least she's a grown woman, not a child," Deacon pops back.

"I'm not a child," Adriana says, her voice breaking as

the tears in her eyes spill down her cheeks. "I'm pregnant, and children don't get pregnant."

Her words hit like a swimming pool full of ice cubes dumped over our collective heads.

My jaw drops, my throat goes whip-tight, and I'm pretty sure my heart stops.

Just…stops, for a long moment, as if by refusing to beat it can keep this from being real. Keep my daughter from being a teen mother, following in my footsteps and making her life so much harder than it had to be.

I was nineteen when I got pregnant with Beatrice and Grant proposed as soon as he found out. But having children so young still drastically altered the course of my life. I dropped out of college, art school seeming a ridiculous luxury when there was a baby waiting for me at home and so little money for childcare. And then I got pregnant with Emily, even though Grant and I were using condoms, and it just seemed like fate had chosen a path for me.

I settled into my role as wife and mother, letting the other things I'd wanted to be fall away. And I loved being Grant's wife—he was so good to me for a lot of years before things went south—and being a mom to my girls is the best part of my life, bar none. But I never got to figure out who I was apart from all that. I went straight from my mother's house to my husband's house. I never lived alone, never figured out what I liked to do when I was by myself, never had the space to dream the adult me into being. Instead, I got to fake it until I made it, pretending I was prepared to be a parent when I wasn't much more than a kid myself.

And Addie's even younger.

So damned young. With her makeup-free face and cheeks shiny with tears, she looks about fourteen. A baby. *My* baby.

My baby is having a baby.

I open my arms and Adriana falls into them with a sob of relief.

"I'm sorry, Mommy," she says, clinging to me as she cries harder. "It was the first time. The condom broke, and I didn't know what to do. I'm so sorry."

"Shh, it's okay." I smooth her hair away from her forehead and kiss the top of her head. "We'll figure it out. You're not alone. I'm here. I'll always be here for you, baby, no matter what."

"I'm here, too. I'm not going anywhere," Jacob says, the words thick with emotion. I look up to see tears in his eyes, too, and my heart breaks all over again.

I nod, lips curving tightly. "Thank you, Jacob. That's good to know, but I'm going to take Adriana home now. We have a lot to talk about."

"I don't want to talk without Jake," Addie says, pulling back to meet my gaze, hers so wild I know immediately we won't be leaving any time soon. "We love each other, Mom. I kept things a secret at first because I knew you wouldn't want me dating a boy in college, but as soon as I turned eighteen, we were going to tell you. But then I missed my period, and we were so worried we decided to hold off, and then I took the test and…"

I nod, swallowing past the lump in my throat as I do the math. "So you've been dating since the summer? Since you were seventeen?"

Addie nods. "I'm sorry."

"Oh, honey," I say with a sigh. "That's the least of our worries now, but you could have told me. You could have told me about the broken condom, too."

"I was too scared," Addie says, eyes filling again. "I thought you'd be mad."

I cup her sweet face in my hands. "Why would I have been mad? Honey, we've talked about this stuff since you were little. I've always told you that I'm ready to help you get birth control or go to the clinic for the morning after pill or—"

"But it wasn't the morning after when I found out I was pregnant," Addie says, blinking faster. "It was six weeks after, and as soon as I saw it on the monitor, I knew I wanted to keep it. I don't care how hard it's going to make college or anything else. I want this baby."

"*We* want this baby," Jacob says.

Deacon curses beneath his breath, the first thing he's said since the bomb dropped. I shift my focus his way to find him standing rigidly in the dim light, tight-lipped and bloodless, looking like he's been dropped in the middle of a warzone under heavy enemy fire.

CHAPTER 25

VIOLET

*A*ddie stands up straighter, her voice shaking but her gaze steady. "I'm three months along. I won't have the baby until after graduation, and it'll be three months old by the time college starts in the fall. And Cal Poly has subsidized childcare for student parents, a great program. I've already done all the research, Mom. The baby will be safe there while I'm in class, and I can study after he or she is in bed at night, and nothing about my plan really has to change."

"That's great, Ad," I say, hating to rain on her parade, but she needs a dose of reality. "But babies are a lot of work, even with daycare to help bear the load. And they get sick so often when they're small. Especially when they're in an environment with other kids every day. And even if the baby's healthy and a decent sleeper, there are times when you won't get any rest at all, when you'll be so wiped out by rocking a teething infant all night that you won't be able to drag yourself to the grocery store for milk, let alone to class. And if you're that far away, I won't be there to help you with any regularity."

"Then I'll go to the store. Or stay up with the baby," Jacob says, chin lifting as he adds in a don't-even-try-to-argue-with-me voice that's one-hundred percent Deacon, "I'm dropping out of school and moving to San Luis Obispo with Addie. We've already decided."

"Like hell, you are," Deacon growls.

"I'm going to get a job, something flexible so I can take off if I need to," he pushes on, his gaze fixed on my face, but his words a clear challenge to his father. "Adriana's way better at school than I'll ever be. It doesn't make sense for her to drop out and lose her scholarship. I'll withdraw at the end of the semester and go back to finish my degree when the baby's older and Addie's in grad school."

My lips part, but I snap them closed again, refusing to let the words on the tip of my tongue find their way out into the world. They're so young, and love is so hard, and parenting is even harder, but Addie's father and I made it work for a long time. I wouldn't trade a single one of those happy years, not even to be spared the pain of Grant throwing everything we'd built together away to hook up with a woman half my age.

Grant...

Oh God, he's going to lose his damned mind.

"I'm assuming you haven't told your dad about any of this," I say. "Considering he hasn't stormed into the house and bricked up the door to your room."

Addie shakes her head fast, her flushed cheeks going pale. "No, I can't tell him, Mom. He'll kill me."

"He won't kill you."

"He'll kill Jacob," Addie says, her eyes beginning to shine again. "And I can't do this without Jacob. I just can't."

"No one's going to kill Jacob," I assure her. "I'll talk to him. See if I can find a way to smooth things over as much as possible before you see him again."

"If she can't stand up to her own father, then she's not ready to be a parent." Deacon's words are kind, gentle even, but that doesn't keep them from making my head explode. I'm about to turn and give him a piece of my mind—a big piece—when Jacob does it for me.

"Back off, Dad," he shouts. "You don't know Addie. She's one of the strongest, smartest, best people I've ever met. She doesn't want to talk to her dad because he left her mom for a girl the same age as her sister, who bosses Addie around and treats her like a kid when it's absolutely not her fucking place."

A year older than Beatrice, but he has a point. One that Grant and I have argued about extensively every time he allows his not-overly-bright and absolutely inexperienced new bride to put in her oar when it comes to raising Addie.

Though, here I am with a teen daughter pregnant by my boyfriend's son, so maybe I shouldn't throw stones.

"I'm not trying to insult Adriana," Deacon says with patience that's clearly forced. "I like Adriana. A lot. As far as I can tell, she's a great kid. But she's still a kid, Jacob, and in a lot of ways so are you. I think it would be a mistake not to consider all the options."

"Like what, an abortion?" Jacob asks, steel in his voice. "Because that's not happening. Adriana and I already talked about it. We can't say what's right for anyone else, but it's not the choice for us."

"Then adoption," Deacon says. "There are so many couples out there who would give everything for a shot at a healthy baby. Especially from kids like you. You're both sweet, smart, athletic and—"

"And we're not giving up our baby." Jacob shifts closer to Adriana, who steps away from me, putting her arms around him and leaning into the person who's clearly well on his way to taking my place as her rock and touchstone.

It hurts a little, to see how far she's already flown from the nest without me even realizing it was happening, but it's also good. Right. If they're going to have any shot at getting through this relationship trial-by-fire, they're going to have to do it as an unshakeable team.

"Please, Jake," Deacon says, dragging a weary hand through his already wild hair. "Can we go inside and talk about this, man to man? I'll give Violet the keys to my truck, she can take Adriana home, and we can all reconvene later." He glances my way, his voice stiff as he asks, "If that's all right with you, Violet. I assume our plans for the day are canceled."

Canceled because we know what Adriana's up to or canceled because *we're* canceled, I don't know. I'm too worried about Addie to stress about what's going on with Deacon and me right now. There will be time to stress about that later, after I've wrapped my head around the fact that I'm going to be a grandmother in six months.

I nod. "That's fine with me. I think Adriana and I

should go home and get some rest. It's obviously been a big night for all of us."

"I was going to be home before you got home," Addie says in a small voice. "That's why we got up so early. I didn't want you to be worried about me. And I had no idea that Deacon was Jacob's dad, or I never would have encouraged you two to…" She trails off, cutting a quick glance Deacon's way before her gaze flits nervously back to me. "You know. But if you're happy, I'm happy. Just because Jake and I are together, it doesn't mean you and his dad can't…be a thing. Or whatever."

"That's gracious of you, Addie," I say, wryly, "but not something that needs discussion right now. First, we need to make sure you're getting solid prenatal care, so this baby has the best shot possible."

"I've already been seeing a doctor. She says everything looks good and cleared me to keep running track. I mean, Alysia Montaño ran the eight-hundred-meter when she was thirty-four weeks pregnant, so I knew it was probably okay, but I wanted to check and make sure. Be one-hundred percent safe." Addie pauses, biting her lip as she glances over her shoulder at Jacob. "We actually have an appointment tomorrow. That's where I'm going at noon. Not to Georgia's house to make Christmas cookies. I'm sorry for lying."

I want to ask her a hundred different questions, all at once—how did she get to the appointments, how long did she plan on hiding the pregnancy from her family, and when did she get so responsible and organized, because I remember a time in the recent past when she couldn't be trusted to make it to the bus stop on time, let alone a series of prenatal appointments—but I'm suddenly tired.

So, so tired.

"I'll take those keys, Deacon." I turn to him, torn between the urge to shout at him for making this already hard situation worse and a wish to fall into his arms for a hug.

"Sure thing. Be right back." He trots across the yard, disappearing into the house. The moment the door slams closed behind him, Jacob's shoulders drop away from his ears and hurt flickers across his features, giving me a glimpse of the scared kid behind the supportive partner he's trying so hard to be.

I put a hand on his arm, giving a gentle squeeze. "It's going to be okay. Your dad is just one of those people who has a hard time letting go of the way *he* thinks things should be. But he loves you so much. He'll come around."

"Probably," Jacob says with a sigh, "but not before he tries to browbeat me into changing my mind for a few months first."

I want to assure him that it won't be as bad as all that—that his dad just wants to make sure he understands all his options and the consequences of his actions—but I'm not sure that's true. I understand where Deacon's coming from, but there comes a point when you have to let people make their own choice, even if you think it's a mistake. Even the people you love.

Jacob leans in, pressing a kiss to Addie's forehead. "Get home safe. I'll be at your place at eleven thirty."

"Do you mind if Mom comes to the appointment?" Addie asks. "It would be nice to have her there."

Jacob shoots a shy smile my way. "Yeah, if you'd want to, Ms. Boden. That would be great."

"Violet, please. And I'd love to. Thank you for including me."

That's all I want—to be included, to remain a part of my child's life as she grows and changes and starts a family of her own. I didn't expect this to happen when she was still so young, and I hate that she's going to have a harder time of things than if she'd waited to become a mother, but she's so precious to me. No matter what path Addie chooses, she's always going to be a person I want to know and love and support, for as long as she'll let me.

As Deacon emerges from the house with the keys, I want to pull him aside and tell him what I know in my heart to be true—that we're here to help our kids get strong enough to make their own choices, not make their choices for them—but his jaw is clenched so tight there's a little marble of muscle rolled up near his ear.

He's not ready to talk. He doesn't want to hear my two cents. And as soon as Adriana and I are gone, I'm sure he's going to tear into Jacob with the unrestrained passion of a man who believes that his way is the right way. The only way.

I pat Jacob on the back, silently wishing him strength. "See you soon. Let's go, Addie." I hold out my hand, palm up, and Deacon drops the keys into it without touching me.

"I'll come get it later. Just leave the keys in the glove

compartment," he says, his voice as cool as the morning air.

I close my fingers around them without looking up, not wanting him to see the hurt I'm sure is visible in my eyes. "Thanks. Good luck."

"It's not too late. We're going to fix this," he says, but I hear what he's really saying.

That *he's* going to fix it. That he will bend the world to his iron will and God help anyone standing in his way.

But I don't think things are going to work out that way this time around. Willpower can accomplish a lot of things, but it can't transform a heart. Love plays by its own set of rules and is every bit as stubborn as Deacon Hunter.

CHAPTER 26

DEACON

Don't go. Stay with me. Don't leave me here alone.
The words come so close to spilling out of me, it's shameful. The only thing keeping them in is my clenched jaw, which I keep locked tight until Violet and Addie pull away.

I've been a single parent for almost two decades and a grown man for even longer. Even when I was married, I wasn't the kind of person who needed my partner by my side for moral support.

I support myself and offer a strong, solid pair of shoulders for the people I love to lean on. I don't fall to fucking pieces, I don't doubt my judgment or second-guess myself, and I don't wish someone else would step in and take the wheel.

But as I face my son across the kitchen table ten minutes later over cups of coffee, I can't help wishing Violet were still here, which makes zero sense. I don't agree with the way she's handling this. She's too accepting, too soft, too easily swayed by the naïve pronouncements of two kids who have no clue what they're signing up for.

If she were calling the shots, we'd already be picking out baby names and stocking up on organic cotton swaddling blankets and vegan baby food.

But still...

I want her here. I want her hand in mine. I want to know what she would say to Jake when he pronounces in a flat voice, "You're wasting your breath, Dad. I'm leaving school, and Addie and I are having the baby. That's it."

They say love makes you do crazy things, but it just feels like it's made me plain crazy. I'm so off my game, my only response is a long tired sigh and, "We should talk about this later. After we've both gotten some rest."

Rest.

The old Deacon didn't need rest or time to think. The old Deacon knew right from wrong, black from white. But now it's all confusing shades of gray, punctuated with questions I'm not sure how to answer.

All I really know as I climb the stairs is that I don't feel whole without Violet.

CHAPTER 27

VIOLET

*A*driana's three-month checkup goes off without a hitch. She schedules her next appointment, and she, Jacob, and I head back to our house for a late lunch, during which I begin to suspect my daughter may have found the love of her life.

Jacob truly seems perfect for her, a goofy, kind, curious, take-no-bullshit person I can see keeping my daughter on her toes—and deeply in love—for years to come.

He stays to watch a movie with Addie and then for dinner after, lingering over tea and cards until both Addie and I are yawning over our hands before he heads back to the farm, clearly not looking forward to returning to his father's house.

Deacon doesn't call. Or text. And I go to bed with a cannonball where my heart should be.

I miss him. So much.

But there's no time to mourn what we had, or what I thought we had.

I have to tell my ex-husband that our teenage daughter is pregnant.

"You want me to come with you?" Adriana asks the next evening, from her place on the couch, curled up under a cozy blanket with a massive bowl of popcorn. "I could hide in the back seat and come in when you give the all-clear signal."

"It's too cold to stay in the car. And I'm not expecting the all-clear signal tonight."

Addie sinks lower on the cushions, worry creeping into her eyes. "What do you think he's going to say?"

"I don't know, but I'm not going to give him Jacob's name. Just in case." I shrug on my coat. "Don't worry. He'll come around. Your dad has his faults, but deep down he's a lover, not a fighter. He won't stay angry for long."

"Okay," Addie says in a small voice. "Good luck, and thanks for telling him, Mom. I really appreciate it."

"Be back in a couple hours," I say, blowing her a kiss as I head out the door, drawing my coat closed at the neck as the bitter wind sneaks beneath my clothes.

Winter crept in like a thief overnight, leaving a chill in the air that insists Christmas will be here before we know it. Best if we get the drama out of the way before then so we can all enjoy the holidays.

Sliding into the car, I pull out, headed for Mama Theresa's.

When I called earlier today to reschedule our Adriana pow-wow, Grant suggested we do drinks at our old local haunt instead of coffee. Usually, I would have said no—there are too many memories at Mama's—but tonight I'm hoping the ghosts of all those happy times will mute the anger explosion.

And memories of the old days don't hurt as much as they did even a few weeks ago. Deacon helped work that miracle, and for that, I will always be grateful to him, even if I never touch his magical peen again.

That's what I miss, I tell myself. The peen, not the man attached to it, the man I was so in love with that my heart feels like it's being pounded with a meat tenderizer.

As I push through the door to Mama's, pausing a moment to let my eyes adjust before moving into the dimly lit bar attached to the restaurant, the smell of garlic and marinara sauce hits so hard I'm overcome with a wave of nostalgia. Not for my marriage to Grant, but for our friendship, the way we'd laugh, and how relatively easy things were then. Back before I knew that even forever love can fall apart in your hands, disintegrating so fast it's hard to believe there was ever any substance there to begin with.

But there was. It was real. And it was good.

And maybe that's enough. Maybe things don't have to last forever. Maybe they were never intended to. Maybe we should all start thinking of love like our careers in this modern world—things that change many times over the course of a life and not the foundation of present or future happiness.

Grant spots me across the bar and lifts an arm with a smile that falls from his face as I slide onto the bench next to his. "Hey, what's wrong?" he asks, voice filled with concern. "Are you crying?"

I swipe at my cheek, surprised to feel tears on my fingertips. "Um, yeah. I guess so. I was just thinking…"

"What were you thinking about?"

"Love," I answer honestly. We're in for a tough conversation tonight, might as well jump in head-first.

Grant's gray eyes, those eyes that were once my safe place, soften with understanding. "Yeah. I've been doing a lot of that lately, too."

I blink faster. "You have?"

"I have." He shifts on his stool, until his knees brush mine, making me flinch. We haven't touched much in the past two years, and the familiar-but-not-familiar sensation is disconcerting. "But I'm sure my thoughts aren't as interesting as yours. You always had good things to say about love."

I press my lips together, fighting tears as I shake my head. "No, nothing interesting today. Just…confusion. Lots of questions, no clear answers."

"I get that, too," he says with a sigh. "How about a glass of wine? Or three?"

My lips curve. "Two. I have to drive." *And stay sober enough to deliver the bad news in the least damaging way possible*, I add silently as Grant orders us both a glass of the house Chianti and water with no ice.

He knows what I like, this man. After nearly twenty years together, he should, but it's still nice. Nice to be known, even by someone who decided that knowing me wasn't as interesting as knowing his new receptionist.

The familiar surroundings, the familiar taste of the wine, the familiar way Grant takes charge—ordering garlic bread and stuffed mushrooms even though I insist I've already eaten—combine to work a little everyday magic. Soon, I unexpectedly find myself enjoying the wine and conversation. We stick to neutral topics, Grant's latest nightmare client at work and the salamander drama at the shelter, saving the hard stuff for later by unspoken agreement.

Of course, Grant has no idea how hard things are about to get, a fact that eventually leads to a conversational stall. I take a gulp of my second glass of wine and push a stuffed mushroom around my plate with my fork, mentally running through the spiel I had all planned out earlier this afternoon.

But now the words feel wrong.

I'm so distracted, so filled with dread, that I'm completely unprepared for Grant to drop his own bomb.

"I can't do this anymore, Vi," he says, hand coming to rest on my knee beneath the bar. "I can't keep pretending to be happy with the choices I've made. I'm not happy. I'm miserable and ashamed of myself, and I regret every second of the past two years. If I could turn back time, I'd do it in a heartbeat."

"Wh-what?" I stammer, my tired brain struggling to keep up.

He leans in, bringing his face closer to mine. "I thought I wanted to be in love again. That epic, crazy, light-your-skin-on-fire love like we had in the beginning." He shakes his head. "But that isn't love. That's just fresh chemistry. What you and I had was love. The real thing. One hundred percent. I was just too stupid to realize it."

I feel my face contort into a mask of what-the-actual-fuck and freeze that way. Surely he can't be doing this to me. Not now. Not here.

But he is. This isn't a dream, a fact he proves as he brings his other hand to my knee, his palms so sweaty I can feel them through the denim of my jeans.

In dreams, people never have sweaty palms. Sweat isn't something that happens in dreams. Neither is garlic breath, but I get a heady whiff of Grant's as he adds in a furtive whisper, "But I'm not stupid now, Vi. I get it. I so fucking get it, but I'm scared to death it's too late."

I'm about to assure him that it *is* too late—even if I still missed him the way I did before I met Deacon, the last of our love died the day he asked me to help Adriana pick out a dress for his wedding to Tracey—but apparently Grant hasn't gotten all his crazy out just yet.

"Tracey's pregnant," he blurts out, his eyes as wide and fearful as Adriana's were when I left the house.

My jaw drops and a wheezing sound emerges as Grant pushes on. "It was an accident. We weren't planning on having kids, never even talked about it. But now she's pregnant, and she wants to keep the baby, and all I can think about is how badly I want to take it all back. Everything—the affair, the marriage, the pregnancy—all of it." He exhales in a rush, drawing my attention to the sweat breaking out on his upper lip. "I don't want to start over with a new baby. I'm almost fifty-two years old. By the time the kid's in high school, I'll be an old man. This isn't the life I want. This isn't what I want to happen. Every night I dream that I'm back home with you and the girls, and then I wake up in bed with Tracey and feel like punching myself in the face."

I sit up straighter, attempting to center myself in the

storm of emotion "Okay. Let's take a breath. Take a step back and—"

"I don't want to step back. I want to lean into making things right with you, Violet," he says, his grip tightening on my knee. "Just give me a chance, and I swear I'll make it all up to you. And if Tracey sees that we're getting back together, maybe she'll change her mind about the baby."

"Change her mind," I echo, my stomach turning as it becomes clear what's behind this sudden hunger for reconciliation.

"Yeah. I mean, I know she wants to be a mother, but she doesn't want to do it on her own."

"So you're going to just…abandon her? Is that it?"

"No," he says, adding in a conspiratorial tone that makes it obvious he has no clue how poorly this attempt at winning me back is going, "but I can make it clear that I'm not going to offer more than money. She'll get child support, and that's it. If she still wants to go through with it, that's up to her, but I'm not going to be there for this kid the way I was for the girls. That part of my life is over."

I shake my head, my lip curling as I push his hands off of me. "I can't believe you. I honestly can't believe you. I thought you were a better man than that."

"Oh, come on, Violet," he says. "Be honest with yourself. You'd feel exactly the same way. You don't want to have a baby now."

"No, I don't, but if a child were to come into my life, I would love it to bits and pieces. Because that's what you do with children, especially your own flesh and blood." I pull a twenty out of my purse, slapping it down on the bar. "The fact that you for one second imagined I would feel differently proves you don't know me anymore. Maybe you never did."

"Violet, wait," he says, reaching for my arm as I slide off my stool. "Stay. Let's talk it out. We could always talk it out."

"I don't have anything else to say to you," I say, before adding in a blunt voice, "except that Adriana is also pregnant, and she's decided to have the baby, and I'll be supporting her in her choice to the best of my ability."

Grant shrinks inside his skin.

"If you have any questions," I continue, "you can email them to me. I don't want to hear your voice for at least two weeks. Maybe three or four."

I storm out of the restaurant, breaking into a jog as Grant shouts from the door for me to wait. But I do not wait. I haul ass like I'm being chased by hungry ghosts.

Then I go home, tell Adriana we'll talk tomorrow after I've had time to decompress, and hole up in my room to eat an entire pint of salted caramel ice cream.

Life, man. Sometimes you have to say fuck this shit and just eat all the ice cream. All of it.

I wake up the next morning feeling like I've been run over by a bus to find two missed calls from Grant and three from Ginny, but only one message. I scroll over to see Ginny's name and my stomach flips with relief. I really don't want to have to listen to Grant's voice first thing this morning.

I got more than enough of him last night.

Just thinking about the bullshit way he behaved is enough to make my head pound even harder. He was such an ass that I feel terrible for Tracey, not an emotion I ever expected to feel for the woman who made it her mission to seduce my husband.

But as I hit play on Ginny's message, all I can think about is Tracey trying to swing it as a single mother while Grant moves on to the next sweet young thing. Or maybe he'll date someone his own age this time. Either way, he won't be sticking around in his current marriage for long. I know that "I'm already checked out" look in his eye all too well.

"Violet, you need to come up to the shelter," Ginny says, her voice pulling my thoughts away from my ex's soon-to-be ex. "I know it's your day off, but you have to see this. The work crew is here, and the brush is almost all gone and, well... I think you should be here, too. Hope to see you soon."

Frowning, I hit delete on the message, wondering what the heck is going on and why Ginny doesn't sound more hysterical about the salamander habitat destruction. Has she already been that radically changed by her new man, her tender heart altered by the hot lovin' of her hunky herpetologist?

On the one hand, I'm glad she's not in hysterics.

On the other, I'm frustrated that so many women let men barge in and make themselves the center of their universe without a fight.

What we want matters. A woman's hopes and dreams and goals are just as important as a man's.

So why do we so often just...give them away?

Well, Ginny may be okay with the not-endangered salamanders meeting an untimely end, but I'm not. I'm not going to sit by and wait for the next big rain to wash out their burrows and send their once hospitable hill-side home crashing down on their little slimy heads. I'm going to do something.

Now. Right fucking now.

"Adriana, I need you to bring me a strawberry-banana smoothie, a glass of water, an antacid, and an ibuprofen," I call out, deciding to take advantage of the solid my daughter owes me for taking the heat with her father last night.

"On it!" Addie shouts from downstairs. "You want dry toast, too? Tammy's older sister says it helps with a hangover."

"I don't have a hangover," I call back, stomach lurching as I swing my legs over the edge of the bed, signaling it might not be finished complaining about all that ice cream I ate last night. "On second thought, yes. Dry toast. Two pieces."

"Coming right up, sweet mama," Addie responds, making my chest ache. She's such a good kid. She's going to be an incredible mother. Sure, she's young, and she'll make her share of mistakes, but we all do, no matter what age we are when we start parenting. But her baby's going to have a hard-working mama with a sharp mind and a solid gold heart. My grandkiddo could certainly do a lot worse.

And I'll be there to help her when she needs me.

But thankfully I don't have a baby to take care of today. My stomach is a wreck. For a few minutes—while I'm taking the world's fastest shower—I worry I might not be able to make it out of the house after all, but the toast, water, and smoothie work their magic. By the time I'm finished getting dressed, I feel human enough to start issuing more orders.

"Can you grab every pet carrier we've got and load them into the trunk and back seat of my car? I think most of them are in the storage shed, right?" I ask Addie as I toss my phone into my purse and head for the fridge, hoping we have something in there that a sala-mander might find tempting.

"Yeah, I think so. I'll check. Do I want to know what you're doing?" Addie asks, heading through the kitchen to the back door.

"I'll fill you in later," I assure her. "I'm in mission mode right now. Time is of the essence."

"Got it," Addie says. "Give me five minutes, and I'll have the car loaded."

"Thank you, baby." I pull open the fridge door, my nose wrinkling at the less-than-scrumptious-looking white baby carrots in the bottom drawer. Do salaman-ders even eat carrots?

A quick web search reveals they do not, and that a trip to the pet store to buy mealworms is in order, which will add at least fifteen minutes onto my travel time. Though, I guess it doesn't really matter what time I get there. The brush is already gone. That ship has sailed. But as long as I get project Salamander Reloca-tion underway before the next storm, all should be well.

I shoot Ginny a quick text—*Be there in about forty minutes. I've got to make one stop on the way. Will you still be around? If not, it's no big deal.*

Almost immediately Ginny responds—*I'll be here. And so will the thing I want you to see, I'll make sure of it.*

What thing? I shoot back.

You'll see when you get here. Drive safe, sweet friend. She closes with a hug emoji and three heart emojis that make me suspect she knows my teenager is pregnant. I haven't had time to talk to her or anyone else—except Grant, of course—but Tristan is her boss, and he's more of a gossip than he likes to admit. If Deacon talked to Tristan, then Tristan likely talked to his wife, Zoey, and Zoey can't keep a secret like that to save her life. Ginny probably took one look at her face and knew all was not right in the friend-i-verse.

For a second, I consider calling Ginny—to assure her I'm fine and steadily improving as I recover from the shock—but Addie is already pushing through the door with a thumbs-up. "You're ready to rock, Mamacita."

"Thanks, baby," I say, kissing the top of her head. "Don't forget to do your homework while I'm gone."

She rolls her eyes. "Yes, mom. I know. I already have it scheduled."

"And your online class, too. Don't forget about it again or your father will have another heart attack."

"It's under control," Addie says, adding in a voice wise beyond her years, "And I think Dad's done freaking out about my grades. He's got bigger things to flip out about now."

"Oh, pumpkin, you have no idea," I say with a sigh, waving Addie off when she starts to speak. "Later. We'll talk about it later if we need to. But I'm sure your dad will want to tell you the big news himself."

Addie's eyes narrow. "Well, that sounds ominous.

He's already called twice this morning. I was waiting until you woke up to tell me if the coast was clear before I answered."

"It's clear enough. Talk to him. And if he refuses to be reasonable, hang up."

Her brows shoot up. "You're encouraging me to hang up on Dad? What the hell did he do last night?"

"I'm encouraging you to stand up for yourself, that's all. Be respectful as long as he's respectful. If he's not, end the conversation. You're both grown-ups now. It's time everyone started acting like it."

Addie rolls her shoulders back. "Right. Good. Then stop reminding me about my homework, Mom. I've got that under control, and I won't be late for the bus again. And if I am, I'll figure out how to get to school on my own. I'm going to adult like hell between now and the time the baby's born. Make sure I'm as ready as I can be to be her mama."

"A girl?" I ask, fighting the tears rising in my eyes. "You think it's a girl?"

"I hope so. I like girls," Addie says, holding her arms out. "And my mom taught me how to raise good ones, so…"

That does it. The tear dam breaks, and I pull Addie close, hugging her tight as I blubber into her hair. Then I have to run upstairs and wash my face and reapply mascara, and by the time I get to the pet store, I know I won't be making it to the shelter in my forty-minute window.

But I'm not worried about it. If Ginny gets tired of waiting, she'll leave. It's one of the things I love about her. She doesn't put up with any shit.

I'm not going to put up with any shit, either, I decide. I'm going to let my hair go gray, embrace baggy linen clothing, and spend the nights I used to go out at bingo. I will make a spreadsheet of every bingo night in the county and become that eccentric lady who plays fifty cards at once and be so busy pursuing life as a bingo legend, I won't have time to miss Deacon. Or sex. Or love so sweet it had me thinking about rolling the dice on happily-ever-after all over again.

By the time I tumble out of the car outside the shelter with two cages in hand and a plastic container of mealworms tucked under my arm, I'm crying again.

And then I circle around the building to the newly bare hill behind the shelter, where all the brush has been cleared away, to see the man I'm crying over loading kennels into the back of his pickup truck.

Kennels full of salamanders.

I know they are, even before I get close enough to see the slimy little critters scuttling around inside.

I skid to a stop in the freshly churned earth, heart skipping a beat as Deacon turns, the pain in his eyes reflecting the ache in my heart so perfectly it hurts to breathe.

CHAPTER 28

DEACON

*M*y hands shake as I brush them off on my pants. "We're moving the colony to the farm. To the hill by the pond." My voice shakes, too. Dammit. I knew I was nervous, but I didn't realize I was a hot mess. I just want things to be okay with us, so fucking bad. "Dr. Bart is going to meet me there tomorrow morning and help get them settled."

Violet stands, staring at me in the fading light, not saying a word for so long my fevered brain starts tossing out worst-case scenarios. She flips me off and walks away, unimpressed with my effort to make things right. She's kind but distant, still too disappointed in me to consider letting me back into her life. Or—worst of all— she looks up at me with those heart-on-her-sleeve eyes and confesses this is simply too little, too late.

And she'd be right.

Sure, I stepped up for salamanders, but I dropped the ball—hard—with my own kid. With her kid, too, which doesn't bode well for a future with this woman who loves her girls with a fierce and tender devotion that makes me wish I could go back and do it all over with the boys. Love them even harder. Softer. Better. Her girls are the center of her world, and unlike my stumbling self, she always seems to know what her children need and has the courage to give it to them—the sweet love and tough lough and everything in between.

As a parent and a person, she outclasses me in every way, but I'm still praying there's a chance for us. I love her too much to give up without a fight. I want a life together, no matter how complicated that life has suddenly become.

Finally, when the silence has stretched on long enough to make my teeth itch, I say, "I'm sorry, Vi. I was an asshole. I got scared and started pushing for what I thought was best and..." I trail off, shaking my head as I hold her inscrutable gaze. "I'm still scared," I confess. "Scared for the kids and for us."

"Me, too," she says softly. "But we're not junior officers further down the chain of command, Deacon. We're your friends and family. And, like it or not, none of us seem to respond very well to the drill sergeant routine."

"Me, either. I almost got kicked out of basic training for popping off to mine." I sigh. "And again, I'm sorry. It's just...a reflex at this point, I guess. When I was a kid, Dad dropped the parenting ball with my little brothers often enough for it to be a problem. As the oldest, I felt like it was my job to step in, and being bossy as hell was the only way I could keep Dylan and Rafe out of trouble." I shrug, chewing on the side of my lip. "And it worked. I rode their asses, and they came home after school without vandalizing property or getting in fights or breaking their arms falling off the ridgepole of a barn someone dared them to climb. It worked with my boys, too. When they were little. I thought they were growing into good men, anyway. But now…" I wrap my fingers around the back of my neck, digging into whip-tight muscle. "Now I wonder if I've fucked it all up from the get-go."

"You haven't fucked it all up," Violet says, her eyes shining. "I don't know Blake that well, but Jacob is wonderful. He's one of the sweetest, strongest kids I've ever met. He knows exactly who he is and what he's capable of, and he learned that from his dad, who he clearly loves and respects so much."

I swallow hard, my own eyes beginning to sting. "You think so? I was figuring he must hate me by now. He hasn't come home. He's been staying at a friend's house in town."

"Of course, he doesn't hate you." She steps closer, bringing her honeysuckle and sage scent with her, the one that will always be one of my favorite smells on earth simply because it reminds me of her. "He just needs you to let go a little, Deacon, to trust him to make his own decisions. I know it's hard. I get it, I truly do. They're so young, and they've got such a hard road in front of them."

I exhale. "Parenting is going to kick their asses."

"It is," she agrees, tone softening as she adds, "But they're so in love. They're all in with each other and committed to being the best parents they can be. And maybe I'm a hopeless optimist, but if any pair of dumb kids has a shot at happily ever after, I think it's our dumb kids."

My lips twitch, but I can't find a smile. Not now. Not yet. "I love them, Vi. Both of them. I hope Addie will forgive me for the way I acted."

She waves a hand, sweeping that away. "You're already forgiven. Addie doesn't hold grudges."

"And what about you?" I ask, easing closer. "Think you can find it in your heart to forgive me?"

"Of course," she says, a tear slipping down her cheek. "But maybe it's best if we go back to being friends."

"Don't say that," I beg, my heart lurching into my throat and sticking there. "Please don't. We're so good together, Violet. You know we are."

"We are, but—"

"And I can be better," I swear, cutting her off before she can take another step down this unthinkable road. "I know I'm an old dog, but it's not too late for me, Vi. I can change. I can back off the drill sergeant routine. I can learn to listen more and closer and harder. I can be a better man."

"You're already the man of my dreams," she says, her voice breaking, "But what about the kids? How can we help them weather all the hard stuff that's coming if we're all caught up in our own relationship drama?"

"We won't be." I slice a hand through the air. "That's over."

She swipes at her damp cheeks with a crooked smile. "Maybe. Or maybe this is just beginning. We could end up crashing and burning, Deacon, and I imagine that would make family events with our grandbaby pretty uncomfortable."

"So we're uncomfortable. So what?" I ask, brows

bunching tight. "It's worth the risk, Violet. At least for me. I'd sure as hell rather spend the next thirty years cursing myself for fucking it up with you than give up now and never know if this is what I think it is."

"What do you think it is?" she asks, hope flickering in her eyes.

I lift a hand, brushing my fingers across her forehead to her temple, the feel of her pulse beneath my fingertips enough to tell me all is right with the world— because she's here and alive and beside me, this woman who has thrown open every door and window in my heart, sending her light streaming in.

"The big one," I say, "the road I never thought I'd find, not at my age, not after being lost in the wilderness for so long." I swallow hard, the ache in my throat spreading to my chest. "You're all I've ever wanted, Violet, and all I'll ever need. I love you so much, baby. And if you'll let me, I swear I'll spend the rest of my life proving you were right to take a chance on me. On us."

Her eyes widen. "Are you…" Her hand flutters to her throat. "Was that…"

"It was, but I should do it right." I drop to one knee in the dirt behind my pickup truck as her fingers come to cover her mouth. "Violet Boden, will you marry me? Let me love you as well as you deserve?"

She blinks fast, her hands still cupped over her mouth, muffling her voice. "I can't say yes. The kids will think we're crazy."

"Forget the kids. This isn't about the kids or anyone else. This is about you. What do you want, Vi?" I ask, praying that I haven't pushed too hard too soon.

She holds my gaze for a long beat, while my heart

slams against my ribs and my palms sweat and my knee starts to ache because I'm twenty years older than the last time I did this. But I know things now that I didn't back then. I know that women like Violet are one in a million, that love is the most precious thing on earth, and that sometimes you have to toss out all of your carefully laid plans and follow your heart.

"Because I want you," I add softly. "Just you. I want your smile and your laughter and your tears. I want the cranky face you make when you're hungry and the mess you leave in the kitchen every time you step foot in it."

She huffs, and her fingers slide down to fist against her chest, revealing the sweet curve of her lips.

"I want you with your hands covered in clay from your latest masterpiece and want you wrapped in a hundred scarves because you hate the cold wind on your neck. I want your thoughts and your fears and your questions," I continue. "Because you ask the best questions. Questions that make me think and feel and realize how much I was missing before I met you. You're the adventure I never saw coming, Vi, but I can't imagine turning back now."

"Me, either," she says, fresh tears shining in her eyes.

"Is that a yes?" I ask.

"Yes," she whispers, setting off an explosion of relief in my chest. "I want all of you, too. For as long as I can get it."

"Thank God." I stand, and she falls into me, hugging me tight while I wrap her up in my arms and hold on for dear life. That was too close. Way too fucking close. "I don't have a ring," I murmur into her hair, "but I'll get one. Tomorrow. Want to come help me pick it out? I want it to be something you never want to take off."

She pulls back, cupping my face in her hands with a smile. "You could give me a ring from a Crackerjack box, and I'd never want to take it off. But yes. And while we're there, I'll get you a ring, too. Mark you as my territory so Busty McChattykins will back off and give you some space to breathe while you're on duty."

It takes me a second to connect the dots. When I do, I grin. "You mean Karen?"

"Of course I mean Karen." She winks. "Poor woman. She has no clue you like women with itty-bitties."

"I just like you. Every part of you," I say, brushing her hair over her shoulder. "Love you. And I'd be honored to wear your ring."

Violet's smile stretches even wider. "God, we're really doing this, aren't we? We're going to get married."

"We are." I nod. "As soon you're ready."

"What about Christmas Eve?" she asks, a teasing lilt in her voice. "I mean, that gives us a couple of weeks to get everything in order. Shouldn't be too much trouble."

"Let's do it. We can elope tomorrow if you want. I'm ready, Vi. I'm not scared."

Her smile softens. "Good. Me, either. But I think we should wait until spring. I want to marry you barefoot on the beach." She leans in, pressing a gentle kiss to my lips with a sigh. "But I should warn you...there might still be drama on the horizon. I went to meet Grant last night, to tell him that Addie was pregnant."

I wince. "I take it that didn't go well."

"No, it didn't. Grant is not on board with being a grandfather and a new dad again at the same time."

"What?" I ask.

"Apparently he and his wife are also pregnant."

"Shit. He's fifty, right?"

"Fifty-one," she says.

I blow air through pursed lips. "I know men start families at that age, but even now, at forty-five, I can't imagine going back to the baby days."

"Grant feels the same way." Her lips curve in a wry smile. "He's so scared he decided it was time to cut and run, leaving Tracey and the baby to figure things out on their own while he and I got back together."

Storm clouds filled with thunder and lightning move onto my face at the thought.

Violet laughs. "Yeah. That was my reaction, too. Not a chance in hell."

"Did he honestly think there would be?"

She shakes her head. "I don't know. But Grant isn't used to rejection. I'm sure it's going to make him less pleasant to deal with than usual. He's going to give us all a hard time—me, you, Addie, Jacob." She motions to the cages in the bed of the truck. "The salamanders, too, probably, just to make life extra difficult."

"I'm not scared of your ex."

"He can be a pain in the ass," she warns. "And I know it won't be easy for you, helping defend the kids' decisions when you're not on board with their choices, either. But they're not going to change their minds, Deacon, and they need us."

I nod. "I know. And I'm going to be there for them. I

217

won't even say I told you so when they have their first new-baby meltdown."

"At least not more than once or twice," she teases, wincing as she brings a hand to her stomach.

"You okay?"

"Yeah. I'm just a little hung over. I only had two glasses of wine, but sometimes that's all it takes on an empty stomach. I didn't eat much yesterday except ice cream. I was too sad and stressed."

"I'm sorry." I take her hand, pressing it between both of mine.

"It wasn't your fault," she says, adding with a laugh. "Or not all your fault, anyway. I'm stressed about the kids, too. Just because I've decided to support them doesn't mean I'm not worried. It's going to be a huge transition. For all of us."

"But we'll make it through," I promise. "We'll all just have to love each other a little harder for the next couple of years."

"I like hard love." She leans closer with a pointed arch of her brow.

"I heard that about you." I cop a feel of her ass, so grateful to have my hands on her again that I can't stop grinning. "I need to go drop some salamanders in my barn, but after that, I'd be honored to make myself available for your hard-loving needs, my lady."

"I'd like to drop some salamanders in *your* barn," she purrs.

"Oh yeah? What's that even mean?" My laugh turns to a hum of contentment as she presses her lips to mine. Damn, she can kiss. Her kisses are the best kisses, her lips the best lips, and they're both mine for keeps.

I'm one lucky bastard. There's no doubt in my mind.

Even when Violet ends up in the bathroom half the night, with what appears to be a nasty case of food poisoning instead of a hangover, I feel lucky to be the person who gets to pull her hair into a ponytail and fetch a washcloth for her head. And when Grant sues her for full custody of Adriana early Monday morning— a senseless waste of money and heartache that will inevitably be thrown out in court once the judge realizes that Adriana is eighteen, an incredible young woman, and more than capable of making her own decisions—I take the crazy in stride and keep on smiling.

I've got a hundred reasons to smile, including Jacob agreeing to apply to a community college near Cal Poly so he can keep working toward his Ag Business degree while Addie starts her freshman year—and the hug he gives me after I tell him I'm proud of him for putting his family first.

I love that kid of mine. And his fiancée. And his brother. And my future wife. She's the best person I know, even when she's facing me down over the breakfast table with fire in her eyes and a white stick in her hand.

A white stick with two pink lines in the window display...

"You've got to be kidding," I say, toast and knife

falling from my hands to clatter onto my nearly empty plate.

"I'm not kidding, Mr. Alleged Vasectomy." Her eyes narrow as she points the test at my chest and takes aim. "Not even a little bit."

I lift my arms into the air, fingers spread wide. "Nothing alleged about it. I had a vasectomy seven years ago, Violet. I swear to God. There's no way we can be pregnant."

But we are pregnant.

Pink lines don't lie.

Violet makes an appointment with her doctor, and I make one with mine, where, after a few tests, I'm informed that my snipped pieces have apparently found their way back to each other, the infamous Hunter family baby-maker refusing to be shut down without a fight.

I apologize to Violet—profusely—over waffles at the diner afterward and promise, "However you want to handle this, I'm on board. Whatever you need from me, even if it's just for me to shut up until you make up your mind."

"I've already made up my mind," she says, looking far more peaceful than she did when she left for her appointment this morning. "The doctor said my hormone levels are great, and I'm in perfect health, and there's no reason I shouldn't have as easy a pregnancy as I had with the girls. At least once the morning and evening sickness wears off in a month or two. So...I'm going to go for it. I'm going to have the baby."

My shoulders sag away from my ears, the relief so intense it makes my head swim for a second.

"But if you're not ready to be a dad again at forty-six, I understand," she continues. "This isn't what either of us signed up for when—"

I silence her with a kiss, a slow, deep, doubt-killing kiss that leaves us both smiling like fools. "We're going to have a baby," she whispers, her eyes dancing. "A baby who will be the same age as our grandbaby."

"We're insane," I say, grin still firmly in place.

"We are," she cheerfully agrees. "And I couldn't be happier."

EPILOGUE

VIOLET

Three years later

The only thing better than a toddler birthday party?

A triple toddler birthday party, complete with pony rides, baby goats, and a bunny-petting area filled with so many beautiful fuzzy things our little ones can't contain their excitement.

"Bunnies!" Nelson shouts for the hundredth time, jumping up and down on chubby legs as Grant and Tracey do their best to clean the goat poo off his hands before he heads in to love on the rabbits. Nelson is *that* kid—the one who always manages to stick his hands in the worst possible thing at the worst possible time—but we love him to bits and pieces anyway.

He's the sweetest half-brother my girls could ask for, and I thank God every day that Tracey managed to convince Grant to pull his head out of his ass and play nice.

She's grown on me in a big way, so much so that I don't hesitate to press extra wipes into her hand as I collect the dirty ones from Grant with a carefully folded napkin.

"Thank you," he says, relief flooding into his eyes.

"No problem." I grin as I toss the wipes into the can by the picnic tables, where my precious grandbaby is still buried in her birthday cake with no sign of coming up for air. It's in her hair, all over her face, and dripping off her chin to stain her pink dress blue and purple.

"Are you having fun playing cake monster, Bella Bee?" I lean down, laughing as Bella flings her hands into the air with a wild giggle.

"Don't encourage her, Mom," Addie says, dodging a flying glob of icing. "Or I'm never going to get her over to the pony rides."

"I don't like ponies, I like cake," Bella announces, as stubborn as her mother and just as beautiful, with her daddy's bright green eyes and raven curls I love to twirl around my fingers when we're curled up for a Nana and Bella nap.

"But you like bunnies, so why don't we go see the bunnies?" Jacob asks, tossing his beer in the recycling can and pressing a kiss to Addie's temple. "Go grab a beer, babe, I'll take over."

"She's not twenty-one until tomorrow," I admonish, earning a jab in the ribs from Addie.

"Keep your mouth shut, woman," she hisses as I draw her into my arms for a hard hug. "I've earned a beer. Finals almost killed me."

"But you got all A's, my brilliant girl." I kiss the top

of her head. "Because you are almost as smart as your little sister."

She laughs and returns the embrace. "No, way. I'm never going to be that smart. Delilah is a genius. An evil genius, but…"

"Lies," I tut, as I set Addie loose to fetch her celebratory beer. "Delilah is an angel. Aren't you an angel, D?"

"No, I'm a unicorn. Don't be silly, Mama!" Delilah, who has formed a deep and possibly unholy bond with a gray baby goat with a black spot over one eye, shouts from the other side of the bouncy house, where she and her daddy are holding a giant bag of baby carrots hostage.

Dash bounds around them, snatching finger-sized orange treats from the goats and trembling from barely-contained excitement. Our rescue pup may only have three good legs, but he's the happiest creature I've ever met and has been Delilah's most devoted protector since the day she was born.

"Clearly, a unicorn," Deacon says, dryly, motioning to Delilah's forehead. "I mean, just look at her."

As usual, my daughter is wearing her hair in an odd braid/ponytail/horn smack-dab in the middle of her head just like Addie did when she was little. But not even her eccentric choice in hairstyle can detract from her cherub face. She's a perfect tiny, chubby, feminine version of her father, from her blue eyes to her wavy brown hair to her surprisingly intense upper body strength, which is presently on display as she gathers her goat buddy under one arm and goes looking for another.

"Make sure she doesn't drop it, Deacon," I say, reaching for the roll of paper towels to help Jacob get Bella cleaned up and ready for the bunnies.

"On it, baby," he says, smiling at me as he trails after the apple of his eye. Delilah has him wrapped around her finger. So does Bella. And Deacon is the best, most devoted daddy and granddaddy in the world.

Not to mention the best husband.

Once upon a time, back when Grant and I were raising the girls, I thought I had it all. And though I wouldn't trade those years for anything, now I know how much sweeter happily ever after can be when you're with the person who was meant for you. We're different in so many ways, but there's no longer a sliver of doubt that I was made for this man and he was made for me, or that Delilah is the best unexpected blessing any couple could ask for.

But I still take my birth control pills every morning. Even though Deacon's doctor swears he's never seen a vasectomy reverse itself twice.

When it comes to the Hunter men's legendary virility, I'm not taking any chances.

"When are Emily and Beatrice getting here?" Adriana asks, falling in beside me as I trail Jacob and Bella across the grass to the bunnies.

"Any minute now," I say, glancing toward the entrance to the parking lot. "They said they were closing the shop at noon." My older daughters opened a vintage dress shop in Santa Rosa last year and are making such a killing they're already talking about a second location in Healdsburg.

"Oh, good," Addie says. "I can't wait to see them. I saved them some cake. Hid it in the cooler in some Tupperware so Bella couldn't get her hands on it."

"Emily will be happy to hear that. You know how she loves icing."

Addie snorts. "Oh, I know. I made sure to carve her off a corner piece." She takes a drink of her beer, sighing happily as Bella rushes the bunnies with a happy squeal. "It's just a perfect day, isn't it?"

"It is," I agree. But I have a lot of those lately, since my family expanded to let in even more love and light.

"Mama look what I've got!" Delilah runs up to me, a baby goat under each arm, making Addie laugh so hard she spews beer onto the grass.

"Amazing!" I kneel down to get a closer look at my daughter's unexpectedly calm captives. "I think you picked the cutest ones in the whole herd."

"I did. I'm going to take them home!" Delilah beams up at me, while Addie mutters, "I told you so," in a lilting tone.

"What did Daddy say about that?" I ask, glancing up at Deacon, who's standing behind her.

He lifts his hands, palms turned to the sky. "Grandpa has been talking about getting goats. Now that Tristan moved his pet cow to his and Zoey's new place."

I arch a brow. "Have you talked to your dad about this?"

"Why would I do that?" Deacon scoffs. "When I could show up with a couple surprise goats in the back seat, turn 'em loose, and see what happens?"

I stand, grinning. "You're a mess, you know that?"

"Nah, just staying open to exciting new possibilities. Just like you taught me."

"You may have learned that lesson a little too well," I tease, but I don't mean it. I love his open mind and open heart.

And his open arms, I love those maybe most of all.

I lean into him, kissing his cheek as he wraps me up tight. "Love you."

"Surprise goats and all?"

"Surprise goats and all," I confirm, and then I kiss him. And I keep kissing him, even when Delilah announces that we're "silly" and Addie agrees with her baby sister, adding that, "Old people shouldn't make out that much. It's not good for their health."

But I don't feel old. I've never felt better, healthier, happier, or more whole than I do right now, with my surprise baby and surprise husband and, yes, even the surprise goats that hitch a ride to the farm in our truck after the party is over.

Ready for more fun & feel-good romcoms?
My Rugged and Royal series is out now!

TURN THE PAGE FOR A QUICK LOOK!

Join Lili's mailing list and never miss a sale or red hot read! Subscribe at Lili's website, www.lilivalente.com.

SNEAK PEEK

The RUGGED & ROYAL Series
The Playboy Prince
The Grumpy Prince
The Bossy Prince

THE PLAYBOY PRINCE
Available Now

**As a rule, I stay away from good girls. To be fair, the
nice ones usually steer clear of me, too.**

But that's exactly the type of woman my grandfather
picks as my future wife. Sweet.
Polished. *Distractingly* cute.

No clue why I'm so intrigued by her.

Yes, her intelligence is a turn-on. And sure, her secret feisty side is fun to rile up. But it's more than that.

If I didn't know better, I'd say I'm falling for the one woman everyone thinks I'm all wrong for.

As it turns out, there's a freaking hilarious twist even I didn't see coming. And when I figure out what my bride-to-be has been hiding, hell, I know I've finally met my match.

I know the world thinks I'll never be more than the playboy prince--I don't give a damn. **There's only one person I have anything to prove to now.**

Her.

CHAPTER ONE
Princess Sabrina Mila Lena Rochat

A woman on the verge of making several
very dumb decisions in the name of love

My family is crazy.

Yes, I realize that, at some point, everyone thinks their nearest and dearest would take home honors at a Worldwide Weirdo Pageant, but in my case, it's actually true.

I run nature retreats for a living, but my real full-time job is making excuses for my family's oddball behavior.

"So, it's okay to take pictures?" The timid woman pushes her thick glasses up her nose, visibly trembling as she shoots a worried glance down the green mountain toward the castle, where my mother apparently retreated after issuing threats to my latest campers that taking pictures would "steal what's left of the kingdom's soul."

"It's absolutely okay to take pictures." I beam my brightest smile to the assembled group of women, while mentally composing a warning to my mother to quit frightening our paying customers.

I know she enjoys regular meals and internet access as much as the rest of us, though she pretends to be a starving Bohemian who can survive on angst and poetry alone.

"I take snapshots all the time for our PicsWith-Friends page. See?" Holding up my phone, I scroll slowly through the grid of literally thousands of snapshots I've taken of the mountain in the past five years. Sunset views from the summit, shots of flower-speckled spring glens, and hundreds of close-ups of local flora and fauna—it's all there, as well as the occasional obligatory shot of the castle looking hazy and romantic in the distance.

Staying on royal land is part of the draw for Camping at Rochat, but our ancestral estate is best viewed from a distance. Technically, I live in a castle—the original medieval main hall and tower still stand—but the building has been added on to by so many generations of eccentric royals that it now resembles a surrealist portrait painted by a deranged toddler.

Up close, the castle's crazy starts to show.

Much like my family's does.

I love my parents and adore my two sisters, but it would be so nice if at least one of them knew how to behave in polite company.

"Oh, those are really good." A taller woman with long brown-and-gray braids leans in for a closer look. "You should be a nature photographer!"

"Thank you," I say, warmed by the compliment. "My father and sister are the real artists, but…"

"Photography is a valid art form," Timid whispers, a shy smile curving her lips. "I like to crochet. Sometimes I go off the pattern and make things up as I go along."

"Wild woman," I tease with a wink.

Thankfully, the joke makes her laugh and seems to put the entire company at ease, which is a relief. The group of ten college botany teachers is my first All-American booking, and I'd love for them to take positive stories about their experience back across the ocean.

"Seriously, you have talent," Braids insists, pointing a stern finger at my screen. "Don't waste it. Like I tell my students—no one will ever see the world exactly the way you do. That's why we need new scientists and artists and all the rest. Each new pair of eyes can change the world."

Touched, I nod. "That's so true. And thank you again." I tuck my phone into the back pocket of my jeans. "If you need anything before the hike this evening, please feel free to text me. In the meantime, get settled and take as many pictures as you want. Of anything you want!"

I lift a hand and back away down the path, a twinge of regret tightening my ribs.

I'd love to learn more about photography and see plants all over the world, but I can't imagine when I'd find the time to take a class or venture more than a hundred miles from home. Someone has to hold this madhouse together.

Especially now that Lizzy is leaving.

Lizzy.

Leaving...

The thought of my older-by-four-minutes sister moving six hours away to a country accessible only by air or treacherous, winding Alpine roads is bad enough. Knowing she's being sold into marriage to an idiot to secure our family's legacy is flat-out heartbreaking.

No matter how much I love this mountain, if it were up to me, I'd sell our ancestral land, put my parents up in a condo, and free us all from the royal ties that bind and gag. But clinging to history and tradition is the only thing that gets my aging father out of bed in the morning, and my mother would die of a broken heart if she knew she'd never get to see one of her girls become a "real" princess.

Since the vote that relegated our family to ceremonial status, without taxpayer support or any power over our country's governing process, my sister's betrothal to Prince Andrew of Gallantia has been the hope my mother's clung to like a sugar addict guarding the last chocolate croissant in the bakery. She's raised Lizzy to believe that marrying Andrew is her duty and destiny, and no amount of common-sense talk from my younger sister or me has been able to change Lizzy's mind.

But we've both tried. Hard.

Especially Zan.

My younger-by-ten-minutes sister, Alexandra, is a fiercely independent businesswoman presently living in Zurich who considers arranged marriage so horrifically medieval that she plans to wear black to the wedding in protest.

Maybe it's the fact that we're triplets that's made Lizzy's fate so hard to stomach. Zan and I know that if the stars had aligned a little differently on that cold December day, it would have been one of us led to the slaughter instead of sweet, shy Lizzy.

But as Lizzy's identical twin—Zan shared a womb with us, but she doesn't share our matching DNA—I can't help but feel it's worse for me. I can sense Lizzy's emotions, even when miles separate us. I know she's miserable to be leaving home.

As I head down the trail, leaving my campers to get settled in their yurts before the guided hike this evening, I catch waves of Lizzy-flavored melancholy wafting up the mountain toward me.

Tomorrow.

Tomorrow, I will lose my sister forever.

Every time I think about it, tears prick my eyes. I've always been a look-on-the-bright-side kind of person, but lately, the sunny side has been hard to find.

I can't bear the thought of my sister married to Andrew the Atrocious.

I only spent one summer with Andrew and his brothers, but that month by Lake Lucerne was enough to make me loathe the Royal Turd. Even under the supervision of the nannies hired to watch over the six of us while our parents and the boys' grandfather drank too much German wine and debated the terms of Andrew and Lizzy's betrothal, Andrew managed to make Lizzy cry no less than ten times.

He thought his pranks—everything from the relatively benign "crickets in the oatmeal" trick to the more brutal stashing of snakes in Lizzy's bed—were hysterical. Zan and I were not amused, of course, but poor Lizzy was traumatized.

She still checks her sheets at least twice before she turns out the light, just to make sure nothing slithery is hiding under the covers.

And no, it doesn't matter that the snakes weren't venomous, or that Andrew was only nine years old. My sisters and I had only been five at the time, and all three of us knew better than to torment other children, and our parents were far more checked out of the parenting process than the Gallantian elders.

Surely, Prince Andrew had been warned by his grandfather to be kind to his future bride and her sisters, but he made a different choice. Sometimes people just turn out rotten, no matter how hard their parents and grandparents try to raise them to be decent human beings.

These days, Prince Andrew seems to be your average playboy prince, rambling around the globe with his brothers, drinking too much, partying too hard, and taking scandalous pictures with half-naked women. But I wouldn't be surprised to learn he's still got a mean streak.

Once a snake-hider, always a snake-hider.

And once they're hitched, he's going to be hiding his snake in my sister.

The thought makes my stomach turn. Lizzy deserves better. She deserves a man who worships her, a man she can't wait to share her life and her bed with.

Which is why you have to do something, Sabrina. Now! Before it's too late.

"But what?" I grumble as I head through the garden and into the afternoon shadows cast by the only home I've ever known. I talk a tough game, but I've never lived anywhere but here, with my parents. I was home-schooled by various nannies, got my botany degree online, and have lived a very sheltered life. I'm unfit to lock horns with a worldly opponent like Prince Andrew.

Or even my parents.

My parents mean well, but they're from another age. They were raised to believe that children should be seen and not heard, that food magically appears at the table without any effort on their part, and that the cash to fund castle expansion and a lavish ball (or four) every year is their birthright.

By the time the royal bank account finally ran dry, my sisters and I were old enough to get part-time jobs to lessen the blow, but my parents have never fully recovered from the shock of learning that the heat would have to be turned off in the west wing for the winter and that there was no money for Brie, just ched-dar, the cheap kind that can be bought in bulk.

The transition was especially hard on my father, a mild-mannered but largely oblivious man who was dressed by his valet until he was in his fifties and literally had to learn how to *put on his own pants* as a full-grown man. But he still awakens every morning and dresses in a three-piece suit from his vast collection, determined to keep the glamour of the old world alive.

He will never be an ally in the fight to keep Lizzy at home, no matter how much he enjoys having someone to talk art theory with at dinner. My father thinks this marriage is a good thing.

And maybe it is. Maybe my mother's right and my mind has been warped by too much modern entertainment. Maybe love is a stupid reason to get married.

It certainly wouldn't have worked out in my case. Thor, my first and only love, adored me, but only until an heiress with a bigger bank account (and boobs) entered the picture.

I often find myself wondering if it was the boobs or the money that sealed the deal, but it doesn't really matter. Thor is gone; I don't plan on taking surgical action to alter the flatness of my chest, and my bank account is perpetually overdrawn.

Living in an ancient castle that's constantly in need of repair will do that to a girl.

As I mount the crumbling marble steps of the back veranda, I find my suited father at his easel, painting the sweeping Alpine view and the quaint village nestled in the valley below for the hundredth time.

"That's lovely, Papa." I pause to kiss his cheek and accept the usual pat on the head.

"Thank you, darling. And how are our guests? Settling in nicely?"

Initially, Papa resisted the idea of opening the estate for tourism, but framing the visitors as guests enjoying our royal hospitality won him over. That, and the steady income.

"They are. We're hosting a group of American botanists this week. They're looking forward to studying the early summer ferns."

"The ferns are delightful," Papa says, his gaze drifting back to the view. "I should paint them soon."

"I'll pick some for you on the hike this evening," I promise, kissing his cheek again, comforted by the familiar scent of oil paint and turpentine clinging to his clothes. I pull in another deep breath, savoring the smell as I step through the open door into the Great Hall and make my way up the stairs to my sister's tower studio.

He might be a little checked out, but Papa is always Papa, and there's something comforting about that. If he's excited about the royal wedding later this summer or sad that Lizzy will be leaving us, he hasn't shown it.

Lizzy's putting on a brave face, too—modeling her dresses for the engagement festivities for the family and helping Mother select gifts for her future mother-in-law —but I know better. I can feel her misery, a dark churning cloud that gets thicker and gloomier with every step I take.

By the time I mount the final stair, the sadness is oppressive.

So I'm not really surprised when I enter the room to find Lizzy lying spread eagle on the floor in the center of a circle of partially dressed mannequins with tears streaming down her cheeks.

"Oh, honey," I say, my heart in my throat. "Just call it off. You don't have to do this. You should only get married when you desperately *want* to be married, not to keep a promise made by your parents when you were too little to understand what it meant."

"It's not that." Lizzy sniffs and drags a limp arm across her damp face. "It's the collection. There's no way I'm going to be able to finish by tomorrow. Not even if I work nonstop without eating or sleeping or peeing."

"You do pee a lot," I say, trying to lighten the mood.

I pad deeper into the room, seeking a piece of furniture that isn't covered in fabric or likely to be hiding a pin that will stick me in tender places when I sit down. My sister is a talented lingerie designer, but she's also a messy artist who thrives in chaos and believes bloody pins help make the magic happen.

"It's because I drink a lot of tea," Lizzy says, her voice quivering. "But don't make fun of me, Bree. Not now."

"I'm not making fun, I promise. Just teasing."

"Don't tease. Help me," she begs, before adding in a warning tone, "Don't sit there. I spilled soup on the cushion at lunch."

I abort my mission with a grunt, managing to reverse the bend of my knees seconds before my bottom hits the chair. "You should eat something other than soup."

"I'm too busy for anything but soup."

"You're too skinny. You need more protein in your diet."

"This isn't helping, either." She rolls her head my way, the rest of her body remaining limp on the floor. "I have to finish, Bree. I'm so close to landing a collection contract. I can feel it in my bones."

I prop my hands on my hips and survey the room. "Well, it won't be easy, but if we start now, we should be able to get everything packed and ready to ship tomorrow. Surely, they have a spare room in the castle for you to use as a studio. I mean, it's going to be your home in a month, so—"

"And when will I have time to work?" Lizzy cuts in. "I'm booked solid with engagement obligations, and I'm sure Andrew will want to spend time together before the wedding."

"He hasn't bothered in the past twenty years. Why start now?" I mutter, not bothering to keep the disdain from my voice.

Lizzy knows how I feel about her fiancé's lack of interest in her life aside from his obligatory monthly phone call and form thank-you note each year in acknowledgment of her thoughtfully crafted Christmas present.

"Because his mother will be there to make sure of it," Lizzy replies. "And I do my best work in isolation, Bree. You know that. So there's only one possible solution."

"And that is?"

"You take my place," Lizzy says, making me snort.

"Yeah, right."

"I'm serious," she whispers.

I snap my head her way, eyes going wide as I realize that she is, indeed, serious.

Dead serious.

The Playboy Prince is out now!
Head over to Lili's website
at www.lilivalente.com
for links and more about the series.

TELL LILI YOUR FAVORITE PART!

I love reading your thoughts about the books and your review matters. Reviews help readers find new-to-them authors to enjoy. So if you could take a moment to leave a review letting me know your favorite part of the story —nothing fancy required, even a sentence or two would be wonderful—I would be deeply grateful.

Thank you and happy reading!

ABOUT THE AUTHOR

Author of over forty novels, *USA Today* Bestseller **Lili Valente** writes everything from swoony small town romance to laugh-out-loud romantic comedies. A die-hard romantic, she can't resist a story where love wins big. When she's not writing, Lili enjoys adventuring with her two sons and puppy Pippa Jane.

Find Lili at…
www.lilivalente.com

ALSO BY LILI VALENTE

The V-Card Diaries Series

Scored

Screwed

Seduced

Sparked

Scooped

Hot Royal Romance

The Playboy Prince

The Grumpy Prince

The Bossy Prince

Bad Motherpuckers Hockey

Hot as Puck

Sexy Motherpucker

Puck-Aholic

Puck me Baby

Pucked Up Love

Puck Buddies

Laugh-out-Loud Rocker Rom Coms

The Bangover

Bang Theory

Banging The Enemy

Saddles and Sin

Diamonds and Dust

12 Dates of Christmas

Glitter and Grit

Sunny with a Chance of True Love

Chaps and Chance

Ropes and Revenge

8 Second Angel

The Good Love Series

(co-written with Lauren Blakely)

The V Card

Good with His Hands

Good to be Bad

The Happy Cat Series

(co-written with Pippa Grant)

Hosed

Hammered

Hitched

Humbugged

Made in the USA
Columbia, SC
06 July 2022

62877392R10143